Falling for Fitz

THE ENGLISH BROTHERS, BOOK #2
THE BLUEBERRY LANE SERIES

KATY REGNERY

SPENCER
HILL
PRESS

Please visit www.katyregnery.com

First Edition: July 2014
Katy Regnery

Falling for Fitz : a novel / by Katy Regnery—1st ed.
ISBN: 978-1-63392-073-6

Library of Congress Cataloging-in-Publication Data available upon request

Published in the United States by Spencer Hill Press
This is a Spencer Hill Contemporary Romance, Spencer Hill
Contemporary is an imprint of Spencer Hill Press.
For more information on our titles visit www.spencerhillpress.com

Distributed by Midpoint Trade Books
www.midpointtrade.com

Cover design by: Marianne Nowicki
Interior layout by: Scribe Inc.
The World of Blueberry Lane Map designed by: Paul Siegel

Printed in the United States of America

The Blueberry Lane Series

THE ENGLISH BROTHERS
Breaking Up with Barrett
Falling for Fitz
Anyone but Alex
Seduced by Stratton
Wild about Weston
Kiss Me Kate
Marrying Mr. English

THE WINSLOW BROTHERS
Bidding on Brooks
Proposing to Preston
Crazy about Cameron
Campaigning for Christopher

THE ROUSSEAUS
Jonquils for Jax
Coming August 2016
Marry Me Mad
Coming September 2016
J.C. and the Bijoux Jolis
Coming October 2016

THE STORY SISTERS
Four novels
Coming 2017

THE AMBLERS
Three novels
Coming 2018

Based on the best-selling series by Katy Regnery,

The World of...

Blueberry Lane

The Rousseaus of Chateau Nouvelle
Jax, Mad, J.C.
Jonquils for Jax • Marry Me Mad
J.C. and the Bijoux Jolis

The Story Sisters of Forrester
Priscilla, Alice, Elizabeth, Jane
Coming Summer 2017

The Winslow Brothers of Westerly
Brooks, Preston, Cameron, Christopher
Bidding on Brooks • Proposing to Preston
Crazy About Cameron • Campaigning for Christopher

The Amblers of Greens Farms
Bree, Dash, Sloane
Coming Summer 2018

The English Brothers of Haverford Park
Barrett, Fitz, Alex, Stratton, Weston, Kate
Breaking up with Barrett • Falling for Fitz
Anyone but Alex • Seduced by Stratton
Wild about Weston • Kiss Me Kate
Marrying Mr. English

This book is for:

Krystle, Jaime, Kathy, Spring, Nicole, Peggy, Danielle,
Tami, JoAn, Brooke, Shari, Debbie, Yenin, Katie,
Dawn, Maria, and Rachel.
You know why.
Thank you.
xoxo

CONTENTS

Prologue

NINE YEARS AGO

Seventeen-year-old Daisy Edwards stared up at the stars as Fitz English kissed a trail from under her ear to her throat, his naked body warm and hard over hers. He assumed she'd done this before, and she didn't correct him, but the truth was, she hadn't. And though she was trying to look relaxed about losing her virginity to the gorgeous college guy with whom she'd been falling in love all summer, inside her heart was racing.

"Are you ready?" he panted into her ear, and Daisy clenched her eyes shut as her nerves threatened to get the better of her.

You can't turn back now, she chastised herself. After all, she'd been the instigator, hadn't she? She'd been the one to leave her uncle's house after midnight and throw pebbles at Fitz's window until he woke up, raised the paned glass, and looked down at her.

"Let's go skinny-dipping!" she'd suggested in a loud whisper, with a beaming grin, looking at his bare chest and rumpled hair. "One last time?"

He'd smiled back at her—that sexy, "we shouldn't" smile he'd been giving her all summer, making her insides run hot and wet as tingles sluiced down her back. He was so freaking hot, she couldn't believe it when she'd caught him checking out her legs the first week of her visit. By the middle of July, he was checking out her mouth with his tongue, and they were meeting clandestinely all over the Englishes' estate, Haverford Park, at all hours of the night.

But summer was coming to an end now. Tomorrow Daisy would be returning to her parents' unhappy house in suburban New Jersey to get ready for her senior year of high school, and a few days later Fitz would be headed to the airport for his junior year abroad in London. They hadn't talked about "what comes next," because there was no next. They both seemed to quietly recognize that their summer fling, no matter how perfect, was coming to an unavoidable close, and there was nothing that either of them could do about it.

"Daisy?" he asked again, his hardness pressing insistently against the soft virgin skin of her thighs.

"Do you have a . . . ?" She swallowed nervously, letting her voice trail off, unable to even say the word *condom* out loud.

"Yeah," he said, leaning over the side of the pool lounge chair to grab his jeans and reaching into one of the pockets. "Are you sure you want to?"

"I'm sure," she whispered, looking up at his blue eyes. They were the same color as the pool water in the moonlight. Dark aqua. Luminous and tender. She could do worse than to give her virginity to someone with dark aqua eyes, someone she loved, after the best summer of her life.

He leaned down and brushed his lips against hers before kneeling on the plastic cushion and ripping open the foil package. Sheathing himself quickly, Daisy kept her gaze fixed on the stars, grateful for the semidarkness that hid her deep blush. He rolled back on top of her, covering her body with his, and she raised her pelvis experimentally, pushing against him lightly, loving his soft groan as she cradled his hardness, as she waffled between feeling ready and feeling terrified.

"You know how much I care about you, right?"

"Mm-hm," she murmured, though she didn't. She wasn't sure. She'd never felt about anyone the way she felt about Fitz, but she couldn't be sure he'd fallen in love with her as completely as she had with him, because they'd never actually said the words.

She had realized only in the last couple of days, as she started packing for home, that she was—for the first time in her life—deeply and terribly in love. Her heart clenched and bled as she imagined walking away from Fitz and getting into her father's car tomorrow morning to be driven home. But she had decided, maybe even against her better judgment, to protect her feelings unless he was forthcoming with his first. Her parents' breakup was going to be tough enough to stomach over the next few weeks. If she told Fitz she loved him and her feelings were left unreturned, the humiliation of his rejection, added to the unrequited nature of her love for him, would be more bad news than she could bear.

She both embraced and resented this newest development in her feelings because theirs had never been that fraught, intense, "I love you forever and ever" relationship so popular among her peers. Daisy was an emotional person, but she was too lighthearted to be happy in a relationship predicated on angst. Their relationship had been built on summer magic. They'd enjoyed each other in that breathless, racing exhilaration of a fast roller coaster on a hot summer night. Watching each other with smoldering looks, holding hands, kissing, touching, learning about each other's bodies, stopping only to share their hopes and dreams. They'd never defined their relationship as friendship or dating—they'd tacitly agreed to enjoy it for what it was, for whatever undefined awesome thing it was. But in Daisy's heart, Fitz had quietly become her everything: her best friend, her boyfriend, and, in a few minutes, her lover.

Fitz was a few years older, eons more mature and more sensible in general, yet from the beginning of their relationship, his eyes would light up at her outlandish suggestions:

Let's go to the local carnival after dark, hop the fence, and kiss on the carousel!

Let's steal some wine and play dirty drinking games on the trampoline!

Let's go skinny-dipping at midnight!

He'd give her that "we shouldn't" grin before grabbing her hand and racing to do her bidding and fulfill her fantasies. It was a huge part of why Daisy had fallen so hard: because Fitz surrendered his rule-following ways to indulge her whims. It made her feel special and even a little powerful that someone several years older and so straitlaced would let his hair down for her. The impetuous teenager and the too-serious college student: somehow they'd fit together like puzzle pieces all summer long, catching each other's eyes, unable to keep from smiling as they simultaneously remembered the things they'd done to each other's bodies the night before. Knowing that he broke rules for her, indulged her, delighted in her—all of it made Daisy believe he was falling in love with her too.

And maybe he was.

But they just weren't feelings he'd actually expressed . . . yet.

"We don't have to do it, Daisy," he whispered.

Yes, we do. Now or never, Daisy. This is all that's left.

"It's been the perfect summer." She looked at his face, reaching up to cup his cheeks between her hands. "I love . . . being with you. I want this, Fitz. I want you. I do."

She berated herself as a coward for backing out of saying what she really felt, but there was still time tonight. Perhaps they would end up *exchanging* "I love yous" in the moonlight after she gave herself to him. Perhaps, her desperate heart hoped, this wouldn't be the end of Daisy and Fitz after all.

He smiled and leaned down to kiss her lips as the tip of his sex pushed against the entrance of hers. She lowered her hands and fisted the nylon cushion beneath her, bracing herself, trying not to tense up, trying to relax and stay in the moment, but she was, in fact, having sex for the first time with someone from whom she would be ripped away in the morning. Relaxed composure was near impossible.

"Oh my God, Daze, you're tight," he murmured against her ear, his breathing shallow and ragged, as he pulled back a little for momentum, then thrust completely forward.

"Oh!" she cried in pain, a strangled whimper rising from her throat. Tears sprang to her eyes and trailed into her hair as her hands twisted the slick fabric beneath them. She stared at the night sky, clenching her teeth so hard, her jaw hurt even more than her suddenly bruised insides.

Fitz froze, his arms trembling on either side of her head from the effort of staying completely still.

"Daisy," he panted, his eyes grave, his voice gravelly with desire and confusion. "Daisy. What the hell is going on?"

She whimpered again, wiggling a little, trying to get used to the feel of his hardness inside her, but it hurt. He was so big, and she was so new at this.

"Daisy . . ." His eyes warned her against lying to him, and his voice was low and serious. "Are you a—"

"Yes. I'm . . . I'm a . . . a virgin."

He licked his lips, still deeply lodged inside her. "Oh, Jesus. You are? Why didn't you tell me? Oh God, Daisy, you should have said something. I would have gone slower. I could have . . ."

He started inching back, and Daisy realized he was going to pull out of her, leaving her empty and alone on their last night together, and she couldn't bear it. He might *not* love her, but she loved *him*, and she wanted this time. She needed it. She clutched onto his hips, curling her fingers into his skin with urgency to keep him in place.

"Stop! Just. Please, Fitz. Don't go. Just let me get used to it for a second, okay? Just stay."

His eyes searched hers, his face a mask of regret and concern as he considered her words. She read his face easily—he was angry with himself, and a little bit with her too. There were probably unwritten rules about being with a virgin, and she'd coerced Fitz into breaking them all by keeping her secret from him. She saw. She knew. But right now, she didn't care.

"Please," she whispered, searching his eyes, the image of her almost-packed suitcase in her cousin's dark bedroom torturing her. "This is all we have left."

It surprised her to see a flash of pain in his eyes, followed swiftly by anger and then by grief. All in the course of a second. She panted lightly, wondering if he would climb off her body and walk away from her into the night, but he didn't. As he stared at her, his face softened with some undefined feeling. Certainly tenderness. *Maybe even love*, her heart whispered.

He caressed her face gently, then leaned down to kiss her again. His lips were soft and firm, his tongue seeking, as his thumbs swiped the tears off her cheeks. He was so gentle, so loving and careful, her body relaxed around him, little by little, until the shock and initial pain of his intrusion subsided. Her fingers loosened their grip on his hips, and she ran them up his back, feeling him shiver lightly from the featherlike touch. He kissed her harder and deeper as she threaded her hands through his hair, finally arching her back to let him know she was ready for him to move again.

He licked her lips as he pulled back slightly, then slid forward into her wet heat with a groan. "Daisy, I . . . I . . ."

"Fitz." She sighed as he filled her, as the nerve endings deep inside her body experienced the deliciously warm, intimate contact with another human being for the first time in her life.

"So good. It's so good, Daisy," he groaned into her mouth. "I want . . . I mean, I want you to know that I . . ."

So overwhelmed by the physical sensations in her body, she leaned up hungrily to kiss him again, lacing her fingers behind his neck and letting her ankles slide up the length of his long legs as he drew back and plunged forward again. She locked her ankles behind his back, and as his thrusts got deeper and faster, a wonderful, warm pressure started building between her legs. She cried out as the first waves of pleasure crashed over her, causing the muscles deep in her body to tremble faster and stronger until they exploded, pulsing around him, contracting and releasing in rhythmic surges. She felt him swell within her, his movements deep and swift, until every muscle tensed and he called out her name, convulsing with shudders before dropping, exhausted, on top of her.

She had no idea how much time passed before she finally opened her eyes to the same stars that she'd been watching before they'd had sex. They still glittered white and silver against the deep, dark blanket of night sky. But they were different now. Just a little different, a little brighter, maybe, and a little farther away.

Fitz leaned on his elbows and smiled, his bright, happy eyes searching hers before he brushed Daisy's lips tenderly with his.

"Let's lie here all night," he murmured impulsively. "Let's lie here just like this until the sun comes up."

She smiled back at him, pulling on his neck to find his lips again, feeling closer to him than she'd ever felt to anyone, knowing with every cell of her seventeen-year-old body that she would never love anyone as much as she loved Fitzpatrick English.

. . . until the sun comes up.

Sometime between now and then, she would tell him. She would tell him that she loved him because she wasn't afraid anymore. They'd just shared the most perfect, most mind-blowing, most profoundly intimate experience of her life. She'd live on this moment as her mother moved out and her father cried and she started her senior year of high school in New Jersey while Fitz's plane flew overhead jetting toward London. And one day—one day—they'd find each other again when the time was right. Deep in Daisy's heart she was sure: *this is only the beginning of Fitz and Daisy.*

"Okay," she whispered against his lips. He grinned at her before pulling out of her body, then rolled to his side to sit on the edge of the lounger and dispose of the condom.

His horrified gasp filled the quiet of the night.

"Oh no. No no no no. Oh God. God *damn* it."

Daisy bolted upright on the chair, reaching for his shoulder, and he turned to look at her, his face a fierce combination of desperation and disbelief. Her heart raced so fast she couldn't distinguish one beat from the next as they combined to create a throbbing, thumping heaviness such that Daisy had never known.

"What?" she gasped, even though she already knew. She could feel it, deep inside her body: the hot, wet evidence of his recent orgasm.

He took a ragged breath.

"It broke, Daisy. Oh my God, it broke."

Chapter 1

Fitzpatrick English walked into the ballroom at the Hotel du Pont in Wilmington, Delaware, stood in the doorway, and sighed. Unlike Barrett, Alex, and Weston, three of his four brothers, who all enjoyed a night out with the best of Main Line society, Fitz wasn't a huge fan of these sorts of gatherings. All things equal, he'd just as soon be at home watching college football in sweats and drinking a cold beer, but Barrett had insisted he attend.

Fitz envied his younger brother Stratton, who had declined invitations to these sorts of events for so long, no one even expected him to say yes anymore. Stratton was probably at home in his denlike penthouse, feet up on the coffee table, glass of Merlot half-finished, and some terrific book on his Kindle. Stratton probably didn't even own a tux anymore. Fitz put a finger into the starched white collar of his shirt and wiggled it slightly, turning the valet stub over and over in his hands as if contemplating a getaway.

"Hello, second-born."

An arm was suddenly laced through his, and he looked down to find his mother, Eleanora Watters English, beaming at him.

"Evening, Mom."

"It's lovely you showed up. I know these things aren't your favorite."

Fitz sighed. "Barrett has a way . . ."

"Barrett has *always* had a way. However, I will say that the last two months have been void of his usual intensity over business, swapped for his intensity over Emily Edwards. It's been a refreshing change to see him madly in love with something other than a deal."

As Eleanora led them through the crowd, toward the table Barrett had purchased for them at the twenty-third annual Kindred Hospital Harvest Ball fund-raiser, Fitz caught sight of his older brother. Barrett always looked like James Bond in a tux, to the manor born, while Fitz always felt a bit like an impostor. He knew all the rules of polite society, of course, but it all felt a little stale after so many years of compliance. He longed for something to shake him up as Emily Edwards had shaken up Barrett. Looking ahead, he saw his older brother, with his arm wrapped around Emily's waist, talking to another couple, who had their backs to Fitz. Occasionally Barrett would look down and smile at Emily, and Fitz almost blushed at the intensity in his brother's gaze. Fitz could barely remember feeling that way about someone. It had been for such a short time, so long ago, sometimes it felt more like a dream than a brief, caustically significant, part of his life.

"Usual cast of characters tonight?"

"Not exactly. The English have been invaded . . . by the Edwardses," she said, forced humor thick in her manicured voice. "Emily invited her parents to join us."

Although she never voiced concerns about her oldest son seriously dating the daughter of the gardener with an eye to engagement, Fitz suspected his mother had had some initial misgivings. However, from the way she looked at Barrett and Emily now, it seemed those misgivings had been exchanged for acceptance. Emily made Barrett happy, and in the end, that would trump anything else where his mother's sensibilities were concerned. She loved her five boys more than anything, and their happiness came first. Though mixing it up socially with one's help wasn't exactly commonplace, if anyone could pull it off with panache, it was Eleanora English.

Fitz looked over the heads of a few guests to see Susannah and Felix Edwards sitting at the table. Emily's father, Felix, the head gardener of the family estate, was in an animated conversation with Fitz's father, Tom, while Emily's mother, Susannah, spoke tête-à-tête with Weston, who was probably untangling some crisis of the heart with their beloved housekeeper.

"I assume nine and ten are Alex and whomever he brought with him tonight?"

"No, dearest." Eleanora stopped them a few feet from the table, and turned to look at Fitz, her eyes careful but searching. "I did say an *invasion* by the Edwardses. Felix and Susannah are practically family these days. They wouldn't exactly constitute an invasion."

Fitz stared at his mother's face, not understanding her meaning. "But there are no other Edwardses: Felix, Susannah, and Emily, that's all—"

Suddenly he jerked his head around to look at the couple Barrett and Emily were talking to. From behind, the woman had long, straight, blonde hair, just like Emily's, that ended in the center of her bare back. He narrowed his eyes, squinting, as he made out the light brown birthmark that looked like a heart, right in the center of her lower back, right over the midnight-blue silk that covered her perfect ass. He had a sudden, blinding flashback to staring at that birthmark over tiny, bright yellow bikini bottoms, and his heart kicked into a gallop.

"Daisy Edwards," he murmured, exhaling the contents of his lungs.

As though she heard him or sensed him, Daisy turned her neck, catching sight of him as her chin rested on her shoulder. His heart slammed behind his ribs as she blinked in surprise, and her eyes widened. Their eyes stayed locked on each other, spellbound and greedy, until Emily said something to Daisy, and she turned back quickly to face her cousin. The ten or twelve feet apart from her was suddenly unbearable, and as though Fitz were made of iron and she were a magnet, he felt pulled to her in an uncompromising way, compelled to move closer to the force of nature that was Daisy Edwards.

His mother's arm, still linked with his, stopped him.

"It was a million years ago, Fitz."

It didn't feel like a million years ago. Nine years had slipped away, and suddenly it felt like yesterday.

"It was for the best," insisted Eleanora.

It didn't feel like it had been for the best. Not at the time, and not now, and not every time he had thought of her between then and now.

"I thought she was in Oregon," he said tightly.

"She was. She's moved back East. Her mother's passed, and her father's all she has left."

"She's moved to *Philly*? Did you know?"

"No," replied his mother. "I didn't even know she was coming tonight. Emily invited her at the last minute when Stratton refused to come."

His breath caught as Daisy gathered her hair in her hands and twirled it once, then settled it over one shoulder, baring her neck to him. The graceful line made his mouth water, made his fingers twitch, made a hundred buried memories fight for his attention.

"Listen to me, Fitz," said his mother, leaning closer to his ear. "There's something else you need to know."

Fitz tore his eyes from Daisy and looked at his mother, commanded by the seriousness of her tone. "You may not have noticed, but she isn't alone."

He whipped his head around, and for the first time he noticed that the man standing beside her was holding her hand, with his fingers laced possessively through Daisy's. His mother's voice was close to his ear and delivered the words he somehow knew were coming, though it didn't lessen the impact of the blow.

"She's come home for another reason, dearest. Daisy's getting married."

He flinched, his teeth drawing blood from his lower lip.

Fitz knew, of course, in a theoretical, vague sort of way that Daisy had her own life, that she'd probably get married one day and settle down. And as long as she was living across the country, out of sight, she was mostly out of mind too. He thought of her often, even after nine years—that gorgeous smile, her throaty laugh, the way her blue eyes followed him and adored him that summer so long ago, the way her bright smile would get him to do things no one else could get him to do. His memories were still sharp from regular perusal—as one might look at an album of photographs once a month—but the barrier of distance had been kind, allowing Fitz to keep any conscious, viable feelings at bay.

Except at night sometimes. If he woke up after dreaming of her, he could feel the phantom pressure of her lips beneath his, the way her pulse throbbed in her neck under his fingers, her bright eyes looking up at his window, *one last time* . . .

And during the day sometimes. If he saw a woman who looked like her, he could be tricked into thinking that Daisy had moved back East and that she didn't despise him, as she'd made clear the last time he saw her. A whole fantasy would unfurl in his heart for a few quiet moments before he'd realize that the woman he saw was not Daisy and the fantasy was impossible.

"I should say hello," Fitz mumbled, and his mother's fingers tensed on his arm again. He patted her hand reassuringly. "It's fine, Mom."

Eleanora smiled at Fitz, her eyes swimming with a hundred unexpressed feelings: first among them, compassion, followed by sympathy and encouragement. "Of course it is, darling."

She was tapped on the shoulder by an acquaintance who stole her attention, and Fitz was left to wander over to Barrett, Emily, and Daisy.

Barrett saw him first, waving him over with a look that told Fitz that whoever Daisy's fiancé was, he was trying Barrett's patience. Fitz kept his eyes locked on his brother, beelining to Barrett's side and leaning over his brother to kiss Emily's cheek. He braced himself before he turned around.

Daisy's eyes slammed into his, still as dark blue as the sky had been the night that they'd—

"Fitz," she breathed in the same throaty voice she'd had at seventeen. "It's been a long time."

She held out her hand, and his eyes flicked to it, wondering what it would cost him to take it and hold it for a second, even in the middle of a roomful of people, even with her fiancé standing beside her. He reached for it, and a bolt of heat shot up his arm from the contact. If her parents were going to choose a name from nature, Daisy had been all wrong for her. Her name should have been Storm or Tornado or Cyclone.

"Daisy," he said softly, holding her eyes and trying to breathe normally. "It's good to see you."

If he affected her as much as she affected him, she was adept at concealing it. She had flinched for a brief second when they first touched, but she'd quickly pasted a polite smile on her face.

"May I introduce my fiancé—"

"Melvin Murray," said the man beside her, and Fitz turned his attention to him for the first time. He was a little under six feet tall, slightly stout, with a cheerful grin spread across his pasty face. "But you can call me Dr. M. Everyo—"

"Everyone does," said Barrett in a singsong voice, like he'd heard it at least three times before. Fitz caught his brother's lips twitch in amusement before returning to the cool facade he always wore, except when he was staring at Emily.

"That's right! Everyone does! And any friend of Daisy's is a friend of mine. Put her there!" he added, jutting out his hand.

It took Fitz a moment to process his surprise before he quickly offered his hand, allowing it to be pumped up and down enthusiastically by Dr. M.

"What kind of medicine do you practice?" asked Fitz, pulling away and subtly wiping the residual clamminess on his thigh.

"Dentistry," said Melvin with a flourish, opening his palms like jazz hands.

"You're a . . . dentist."

"Yessiree. The best one in Portland until this little hunk of heaven told me she was moving back to Philly. Well, don't you know, I popped the question then and there so's I wouldn't lose her. And you know what?"

"I can't imagine."

"Now I'm going to be the best dentist in Philly!"

Fitz flicked his eyes at Daisy—Daisy the living goddess, sex-on-a-stick Daisy, draped in midnight blue—who stared deferentially at her buffoon of a fiancé like he was the best thing since sliced bread.

"Mel," said Daisy in her honey voice, placing a hand on Melvin's forearm, and damn it if Fitz didn't actually feel the quick sting of jealousy for pasty, paunchy Dr. M. "I need you alone for a minute."

Melvin waggled his eyebrows at Fitz before allowing himself to be pulled away by Daisy.

As they crossed the ballroom, headed for the lobby of the hotel, Daisy tried to quiet the fierce beating of her heart. Everything was going according to plan.

She'd done it. She'd seen Fitz English, and she had managed not to fall over, faint, or throw herself at him like a groupie. The money she'd spent on her new ball gown had been well worth it too, from the way his jaw dropped when he saw her. She looked nothing like the pathetic girl she'd been the last time he'd laid eyes on her. She was all grown up: quietly successful, engaged, and mature.

Yes, everything was going according to plan except . . . Josh.

As soon as they were in a dark, quiet corner of the lobby, Daisy turned to her acting partner in a flurry.

"What the hell, Josh?"

He cringed. "Too much?"

"*Too much!* Not to mention, you're channeling the biggest dork who ever lived."

"Hey. I *am* a dentist, Daisy."

"I know." She sighed.

"And I'm a very good dentist."

"You *are*," she insisted, giving him a sheepish smile. Josh was very sensitive, *and* he was doing her a huge favor. She needed to be kinder to him.

"A lot of people don't respect the profession of dentistry, and if that's the—"

"*I* do. I respect it very much, Josh."

"I was trying to be funny and successful. Aren't other guys threatened by funny and successful?"

Daisy rolled her eyes. "Actually, they're threatened by debonair and sexy."

"Well then, you should have asked Ted to come to Philly with you," said Josh, pouting. "I play the second banana, not the leading man."

Ted was another actor in their community theater group back home, in Wilbur, Oregon, and Daisy *had* asked Ted to join her for the weekend, but at the last minute he canceled, due to real-life work commitments. With two airline tickets already purchased, Daisy had turned to Josh, a good friend whom she'd known for years. But Josh was right—he wasn't really leading man material. With a slight beer belly, thinning hair, and the beginnings of jowls, he was the very definition of *unthreatening*.

"Listen, you don't have to threaten anyone, Josh. I just couldn't bear to come home single, looking pathetic and alone. Could you just tone it down? A little? And maybe try to be . . . sexier?" She cringed as she said it.

"It's not my strong suit, but I'll try. Any suggestions?"

"Keep your arm around me or your fingers laced through mine. Maybe brush my hair from my shoulder and kiss my neck. You know, like we're in love."

Josh nodded, his eyes trained on hers as she gave him notes on his performance. Josh took notes very seriously. "Yep, yep. I see where you're going here."

Daisy nodded, smiling in encouragement. "You know, run your finger down my arm, or, um, maybe say something about *later*." When she said *later*, Daisy used air quotes. "You know, like, um, 'I can't wait to get you alone *later*.' Something like that."

"Ohhhhhhh," said Josh, tsking, then nodding slowly, like the mysteries of the world were being revealed. "You know, Daisy? I should try some of this stuff on Sara Meyers when we get back."

Daisy lurched forward, smiling and placing a hand on Josh's arm. "Yes! That's a great idea. Pretend I'm Sara. And you're trying to seduce me. Like Stanley in *A Streetcar Named Desire*."

"Oh," said Josh, his face falling. "Stanley was Ted's role."

"But you *could have* done it, Josh. You have the talent. Definitely."

"You think?" He perked up again.

Good Lord, being an acting coach was exhausting. She was glad she was a baker instead.

"Of course! Pretend I'm Sara playing Stella." She tossed her hair in an attempt to be sexy. "And you be my Stanley. All manly and gruff and sexy, okay? That's the scene."

Josh took a deep breath and nodded. "Got it. You leave it to me, *Stella*."

He winked, then closed his eyes, wringing out his hands and hopping up and down. She'd seen Josh do this before. He was getting into character.

Daisy looked over her shoulder to be sure no one was watching them. When she was content that their charade was safe, she turned back to Josh, who had opened his eyes. They were focused, with hunger and precision, on Daisy.

"Come on, baby," said Josh, putting his arm around her waist and pulling her up against his side possessively. "Let's roll."

When Daisy and Dr. M. returned, her hair was slightly messy and her lipstick had been reapplied. Not to mention, the goddamned dentist's beefy hand was clutching the bare skin of her hip like he owned her. Fitz's fingers curled into fists, and he exhaled through his nose like a bull.

"I hope you didn't wait for us," said Daisy, taking a seat at the table between Fitz and Barrett.

"Dr. M. has needs," said Dr. M. in a growl, leaning down to push her hair to the side and press his puffy lips to the side of her neck. He narrowed his eyes meaningfully at Fitz before taking his seat across the round table between Susannah and Emily.

Fitz looked askance as Daisy picked up her preset dinner wineglass and took a long sip. What was she doing with this guy, anyway?

As she replaced the glass, Fitz picked up his, and their wrists brushed. He froze, and when he looked at her, she was staring at the place where their skin touched, mesmerized.

"Daisy," he said softly, not daring to move. "It's a surprise to see you again."

She withdrew her hand quickly, placing it in her lap and looking up at him. "It's been years."

"How have you been?"

As the light buzz of polite conversation surrounded them, Fitz sipped his wine, turning his body slightly to face her. Convention required a girl-boy-girl-boy pattern for sitting down to dinner, and Fitz had jockeyed heavily to keep the seat between him and Barrett empty for Daisy.

"Fine. Busy."

"What do you do now?"

She sat back in her seat, looking at him through darkened lashes. She was wearing mascara. He knew this because he remembered that her lashes were as pale as her hair.

"I bake cookies."

"*What*?" he asked, taken aback, distracted from her eyelashes.

She grinned and nodded. "I own a company called Daisy's Delights. I make cookies and decorate them and sell them online."

"Cookies." It sounded so wacky, and yet somehow it was perfect.

"What can I say? People like my cookies."

He could tell she hadn't meant for her words to be suggestive, but he flicked an approving glance to her breasts anyway. Her eyes widened in surprise as she perceived his meaning, and she shrugged delicately, making the halter of her dress ripple lightly in the dim light of the ballroom. He longed to lean forward and press his lips to her shoulder, trail them up her warm skin to her throat, and rest them on her fluttering pulse. Was she remembering as he was? Now that she was sitting here beside him over nine years later . . . was she remembering the night by the pool? All the nights that went before, when he touched her, loved her, made her come beneath his fingers?

"I'm sort of sick of the online thing, though," she continued quickly, her voice slightly more nervous than it had been before. "I think what I'd really like to do is have a little brick-and-mortar shop. Still called Daisy's Delights, but a smart little bakery. With cupcakes and cookies and really good coffee."

"Why don't you do it?"

"Oh, I wouldn't know the first thing about getting started," she said. "Someday I will. Maybe."

Fitz filed this away. If there was anything the English brothers were good at, it was business. If Daisy wanted to start one, he would help her. It was the least he could do if her fiancé wouldn't.

"Couldn't, uh . . ." Fitz flicked his glance at Melvin, who sat with his arms crossed over his chest belligerently, staring at Daisy from across the table. "Couldn't Dr. M. give you a hand?"

"I suppose he could," she said, looking at her beloved, who scowled back at her. She turned to Fitz. "But I've never told him about it."

Fitz frowned at her. What kind of guy was he anyway? She didn't share her dreams with him? Was she afraid of him? The aggressive way he stared at her now had Fitz on his guard. Had she told Melvin about their history? That might account for the angry, possessive looks he kept shooting at them.

"Well, if you ever need any help . . . ," said Fitz vaguely.

"If I need help, then what?"

Fitz flicked a glance back to Melvin, who tore off a piece of bread with his teeth, chewing slowly as he stared at Daisy with barely concealed menace. Was he bipolar or something? One minute he was making dumb jokes about proposing to Daisy, and the next he was scowling at her like a jealous lover. Man, Fitz didn't like this guy. She deserved better. Way better. After what she'd been through, Daisy deserved the best.

"Then I'd be happy to help you. Any of us. Alex is a whiz with money. Weston's about to take the bar. Stratton can research real estate. And it's well known that Barrett's the shark of English & Sons."

"And you?" she asked, her throaty voice sending darts of pleasure to his groin, which flexed and released, waking up to the almost-forgotten sound of Daisy Edwards. Daisy, who'd had him under her spell, in a walking daze from the very first moment they met.

"Daze," he said quietly, picking up his wineglass again and seizing her dark blue eyes over the rim without smiling. "I'd do anything for you."

Chapter 2

I'd do anything for you.

The words hung between them, thick and heavy, as the world around them slipped away.

Daisy stared, her mouth and eyes soft, her heart thumping with longing.

If it was possible, he was more beautiful than he'd been that summer. He'd been superhot at twenty, but at thirty, he was a man. Tall and blond, with those amazing blue eyes and crazy-beautiful cheekbones. His chest was broader, but his waist was trim, and she remembered what his hips looked like underneath his tux—a mouth-watering V of contoured muscle pointing the way to heaven. And she still remembered what it felt like to feel that hot, hard part of his body inside hers.

For years, Daisy had waited for him to come to her—waited to hear from him again, for him to tell her that it didn't matter if she hated him, it didn't even matter that she didn't want him—he still wanted *her,* and the strength of his love was enough for both of them. But the years had passed, and he hadn't come. And he'd certainly never told her that he loved her.

After what had happened, her parents insisted she needed a fresh start, and she'd been whisked out to San Francisco to live with her mother and finish the rest of high school there. After which she'd attended a culinary school in Napa Valley. Following her tall, blond-haired, blue-eyed boyfriend, Glenn, to Oregon, she'd started baking cookies to help pay the rent. By the time Glenn had skipped town with a friend from Daisy's acting group, saying he was finished playing the part of stand-in for whomever it was Daisy couldn't get over, she was making a decent income with the cookies. She kept baking, her only real extracurricular pleasure the theater group, which allowed her the relief of being someone else for a few nights every year. It was a balm to the loneliness of who she actually was.

When Emily called two months ago with the news that she and Barrett English had finally gotten together, Daisy's brain had been flooded with memories of the summer she'd spent at Haverford Park with her aunt, uncle, and cousin as her parents worked out the details of their divorce. But mostly her memories were of Fitz, and with those memories came the realization that Glenn was right. In all her fantasies, Fitz English was still the leading man. Pathetically, despite Fitz's apparent disinterest in her, despite the years that had passed, she wasn't over him, and she would never *be* over him unless she deliberately took steps to get him out of her system. She just couldn't figure out how to do that from three thousand miles away.

When Daisy's aging father had called her a few weeks later to share that he was moving from New Jersey to Haverford, Pennsylvania, to be closer to his brother Felix, he'd also swallowed his pride and asked if Daisy had any plans to return East. She decided then and there: it was time to go home. It was time to stop running, to deal with her useless feelings of love for a man who'd never loved her back. And hopefully, once she'd let go of Fitz English once and for all, her heart would be free to find someone else to fill the loneliness in her life. Because that was what Daisy wanted most of all—to be loved and love someone in return.

I'd do anything for you . . .

She looked at his austere face, which showed no trace of affection for her, and she finished the sentence for him in her head:

. . . because I still feel so damn guilty about my part in what happened.

Suddenly the spell was broken, and she heard the low buzz of the room again—conversations and laughter and the tinkling of silverware and glasses.

She cleared her throat, looking across the table at Josh, who licked his lips at her and narrowed his eyes at Fitz. Daisy grimaced. He was taking this Stanley Kowalski thing a little too seriously. Still, it was better than the hail-fellow-well-met dentist shtick. At least this way she looked desirable to *someone* on the face of the earth.

"When's the happy day?" asked Fitz, his voice dry with derision.

She turned from Josh to look into Fitz's dark aqua eyes. "We haven't set a date yet."

"You're not wearing a ring either."

"He hasn't given me one yet."

"Has he asked you to marry him *yet*?" asked Fitz with a snort.

"Yes, he has." Her eyes flashed. "And I said yes."

Fitz's eyes narrowed and he huffed, crossing his arms over his chest and looking away. "Should've given you a ring."

"This judgment from your vast experience with proposing?"

She was trying to be sarcastic and light, but his eyes cut to hers, quick and furious, and she realized what she'd said a second too late.

"I've only been engaged once in my life, Daisy."

Her cheeks flushed hot, and she could feel the color creeping up her neck, into her face, until she was sure she was beet red.

"You know better than anyone that it didn't work out."

She'd been holding her breath, but her lungs ached, so she let it out slowly, letting the hot air blow past her dry lips raggedly. Her plan certainly wasn't going very well.

Fitz, from whom she'd expected very little tonight, was coming through for her with flying colors. While he was utterly gorgeous, he was also terse, borderline belligerent, and patently uncomfortable sitting beside her. He'd probably gone to the bathroom for a moment only to come back and groan that he'd been trapped into sitting next to her for dinner.

And yet, for Daisy, their history felt more alive than it had in a decade, swirling around her with the conflicting feelings of sun-kissed summer lust, unforeseen disaster, and furious recrimination. Her attraction to him, it seemed, was unchanged and just as charged, despite what had happened nine years ago and the nine years that had lapsed without any contact. Every time he shifted in his seat, she panted. When their skin touched, long dormant muscles deep inside her body pulsed with recognition and need. She wanted him just as much now as she had that night by the pool, just as much as she had every time she allowed herself to think about him since, which was pathetically often. She took another sip of wine, unable to eat anything with a million butterflies in her stomach.

And all he felt for her, as far as she could tell, not counting the way his eyes had quickly checked out her "cookies," was some leftover, misguided sense of obligation. Maybe if she could steer the conversation to safer waters, she could somehow reassure him that he didn't owe her anything.

"Let's leave the past in the past, shall we?" she finally said softly, swallowing the wine over the lump in her throat.

"Fine," he said, sitting back from the table as his untouched salad was cleared away.

She might make him uncomfortable, but they shared family in common—or would soon, thought Daisy, catching a loving look between Emily and Barrett. They needed to get past this awkwardness so that when they occasionally ran into each other at events, like Emily and Barrett's inevitable wedding, or when she was visiting her aunt and uncle at Haverford Park, their past wouldn't haunt them both. She was willing to offer as much polite conversation as it took to get them there.

She fixed a bright smile on her face and turned to face him. "So, what about you? What have you been up to?"

"I work at English & Sons," he said tersely.

"You were pre-law the last time I saw you."

"I got my JD," he said, indicating that he'd finished his legal studies. "I'm the chief compliance officer for the company now."

"So fancy," she said, trying to keep her tone light, despite the fact that he was refusing to look at her.

"Just making sure we don't go to jail."

"Would that be likely? What kinds of illicit deals are you guys doing, anyway?"

He released a quick, surprised chuckle and turned to her, looking so much like the Fitz she'd fallen in love with, it broke her heart a little. His lips tilted up just a touch, as they used to when she surprised him with some outlandish idea, and they'd banter back and forth before he agreed to go along with it.

"Wouldn't you like to know?" he asked, searching her eyes like he was remembering something from a long time ago.

"Oh, I would," she said, an old rhythm coming easily to their conversation.

"It's *very* scintillating."

She tried not to grin back but couldn't help herself. "I'm all ears."

"We buy companies," he said, pressing a finger to his lips like he was sharing a secret.

"Companies! The mind reels. Edgy stuff?"

"Oh, very. Shocking, even."

"Do tell!" she demanded, trying not to giggle, but the happy, alive feeling bubbled up inside her anyway.

"We may—or may not—dabble in . . . *shipbuilding*."

He said it conspiratorially, and she put her hand over her heart, pretending to gasp. "Not shipbuilding! Oh, the humanity!"

"Yes. And sometimes? *Steel manufacturing*."

"Be still my beating heart! The glamour, the . . . the excitement!"

He chuckled lightly, like he didn't enjoy himself very often, and this was the most fun he'd had in ages. "And once in a while . . . Are you sitting down?"

"I am."

"Hold on to your seat." He was trying not to laugh and finally won the fight to take himself very seriously. He looked grim and important as he announced, over-enunciating every word, "Once in a while, we buy . . . *human resource software.*"

Emily put the back of her hand to her forehead and pretended to faint against the back of her chair. Fitz's voice was soft in her ear a moment later.

"Shall I get Dr. M. over here to give you mouth-to-mouth?"

She turned her head toward his voice, but didn't give him a chance to lean away first, and his lips brushed softly across her cheek as she faced him. When she opened her eyes, his mouth was inches from hers, and she could feel the heat of his breath on her skin.

How about you *give me mouth-to-mouth instead?* she thought, flicking her eyes to his lips. She must have inadvertently telegraphed her thoughts because he sucked in a breath as his eyes dilated and darkened.

He leaned away from her sharply, placing his hands on the table and staring at them as if he needed to know exactly where they were to be sure they didn't misbehave.

She gulped softly, taking a deep breath and sitting up straight in her chair.

"You always were fun," he conceded quietly.

"So were you," she answered, and without thinking she placed her hand over his.

She touched him because their bantering had reminded her of the best parts of falling in love with him. She touched him because he was her first love, and somewhere deep inside she *still* loved him. She touched him because not touching him when he was finally so close to her after so long was almost unbearable.

Almost immediately he flipped his hand so they were palm to palm, flush against each other. As he laced his fingers through hers, he looked up slowly to meet her eyes.

He flinched at what he saw there. "Daisy. Daisy, I'm so damned—"

"I like *this*," said Josh, who was suddenly standing in the space between their chairs. He reached for Daisy's hand and jerked it away from Fitz's, depositing it in her lap, then shoved his face into hers until they were nose to nose. "Holding hands with some other guy on the side, eh?"

"Jo—*Honey*," said Daisy softly, surprised by Josh's sudden appearance and his commitment to the role he was playing. "It isn't what you think. We're just old frie—"

"What I *think*? Are *you* going to tell me what *I* think?"

She tried to signal him with her eyes that he was getting a little too over-the-top, but Josh and Stanley Kowalski had become one. She peeked around Josh for a second to check out Fitz's reaction, but all she could see was Fitz's hands on the table. He had one hand fisted inside the other, cracking his knuckles. Then he switched and did the same with the other hand.

Daisy's mind reeled. Fitz wasn't actually priming himself to *hit* Josh, was he?

That would mean he felt protective of her, or jealo—*no*, she told herself, before her silly fantasies got the better of her. He didn't care about her like that. He didn't see her like that. Her confusion translated to furrowed brows and quickened breaths, and Josh leered at her in character.

"Scared'a me? You *should* be," said Josh in a menacing tone, winking at her.

"I swear to God, if you don't back away from her on your own, I will make you." Fitz's voice was smooth and low behind Josh, cracking like a soft whip with its fierce intensity.

Josh winked at her again, then leaned back to look at Fitz with derision, still channeling Stanley Kowalski with aplomb. "You and what army?"

Fitz stood up so fast, his chair hit the ground behind him, swiftly followed by Josh, who took a quick, hard jab to the nose and fell to the floor.

"What the hell, Fitz?" demanded Barrett, standing up beside Daisy's chair.

Daisy gasped, sliding off her seat and onto her knees, reaching for Josh, who was covered in blood and practically in tears. "That was assault. He might'a broke my nose."

Breathless and confused, Daisy looked up at Fitz with wide eyes.

Fitz ran his hands through his hair, then opened them to her in supplication. "I don't—I don't like the way he talks to you!"

That declaration snapped Daisy out of her trancelike state.

"Well then, by all means, hit him." She shook her head. "When did you turn into a Neanderthal, Fitz?"

They'd attracted quite a little crowd by now, Barrett helping Josh get to his feet, and Emily coming around the table to take Daisy's arm and help her off the floor. Emily pursed her lips and stared at Fitz in disbelief, then put her arm around her cousin's waist.

"This isn't like you, Fitz," Emily exclaimed with wide, shocked eyes.

Fitz's jaw looked like it was about to pop from the way he was clenching it, and his eyes, which were wild and furious, didn't let go of Daisy's even as Emily berated him. It was almost like he was seeing her for the first time, and Daisy's whole body prickled with awareness.

Barrett was helping Josh to the bathroom, and Emily directed their course to follow. Daisy looked back once, just in time to see Fitz pick up the chair he'd knocked over and stalk out of the ballroom without a second glance.

Fitz gave his valet ticket to one of the uniformed guys outside, then paced the curb, trying to figure out what the hell had just happened.

Daisy Edwards, that's what.

The summer they spent together had practically been defined by the way she got him to do things he'd never consider doing on his own: breaking and entering, public nudity, trespassing . . . In his whole life, only Daisy had ever had that effect on him. She made him so nuts, it was like he'd do anything for her.

All Fitz knew was that the minute that asshole had jerked her hand out of his, it took every ounce of self-control Fitz possessed not to deck him. And then finally, he snapped. For God's sake, he'd *threatened* her, telling her she should be scared of him. He deserved to have his lights punched out. Fitz highly doubted he'd broken anything, but a broken nose was too good for Dr. M. He deserved a broken head for mistreating the sexiest, funniest, most beautiful girl in the world.

The valet pulled up with his Mercedes CLS-Class silver sports car, and Fitz stomped to the driver's side, giving the valet a twenty before plopping down in the supple leather seat. It felt good stepping on the gas, but Fitz didn't want to go home. If he did, he'd probably just end up getting drunk, remembering the curve of Daisy's neck in that ridiculously skimpy dress, the way her cheek felt beneath his lips as she'd turned her head, the way her eyes had looked when she'd taken his hand. Jesus. Nine years had gone by and he still wanted her just as much as he had that summer. He slammed his hand on the steering wheel once, twice, *threefourfive* times, until the heel of his palm ached.

He certainly hadn't expected to see her tonight. Frankly, he'd never expected to see her again, and then there she was in the Hotel du Pont ballroom out of the blue—still so unbelievably beautiful, so sexy and vivacious, making him laugh about the boring deals he worked on every day, making his blood rush like wildfire and his body harden with want for the slightest touch. That was the thing about Daisy: being around her was like a drug to Fitz. It felt so good, so exciting and exhilarating, it was like he'd do anything to hold on to that feeling. It made him foolish and imprudent. So much so that he'd actually hit her fiancé. *Hit* him. Fitz groaned, shaking his head, furious with himself.

After half an hour of self-criticism and rebuke, he found himself pulling up outside Stratton's apartment building. He found a parking spot and crossed the street, nodding to the familiar doorman and using his spare key to take the reserved elevator all the way to the top floor. Once there he knocked on Stratton's door, then unlocked it himself.

If Stratton was thrown off by an impromptu guest at ten-thirty, Fitz wouldn't have known. He barely saw his brother's face as he beelined past him to the kitchen, opened the fridge, took out a bottle of Stella Artois, and proceeded to chug the whole thing. Then he opened another, placed it on the counter, and tugged at his bow tie. Stratton sauntered into the kitchen a minute later and found Fitz halfway through the second bottle of beer.

"Wow. Good time tonight?"

Fitz shook his head, taking another sip, then brushed past Stratton, shrugging out of his tux jacket and flopping onto the black leather couch with an exhausted sigh. "No."

Stratton reached down for the remote and turned off the TV, then sat down in a black leather chair facing Fitz.

Fitz looked up, grateful for the quiet refuge of Stratton and his apartment. While Barrett was sternly commanding, Alex was a man-whore playboy, and Weston was the attention-seeking youngest, Stratton was socially awkward but quiet, intense, and thoughtful. Fitz loved all his brothers, but in moments of personal crisis, Stratton was his go-to man.

Fitz ran his hands through his hair. "I punched a guy in the face, Strat. At the gala. I . . . I punched him."

Stratton's eyes bugged out of his head behind his glasses, and he leaned forward, resting his elbows on his knees. "*You*? What the hell? What happened?"

"Do you remember Daisy Edwards?"

"Vaguely. Felix's niece, right?"

Fitz nodded. "She stayed with Felix and Susannah the summer she was seventeen. I was twenty, almost twenty-one. We—we were together."

"I don't remember this. Like how?"

"Like, I was crazy about her, and we fooled around all summer on the sly."

"Oh. Wow, really? Huh. Why on the sly?"

Fitz shrugged. He didn't have a good answer other than the excitement of it. Their secret love affair felt illicit. Risky. Everything Fitz wasn't, and yet he'd loved every second with her.

"I don't know. That's just the way it was."

"Okay. Then what?"

Fitz reached for his beer and took a long swig, hoping it would numb him a little, but it didn't help. He hadn't articulated the details of that summer to anyone for a very, very long time. In fact, aside from Daisy, his mother was the only person who even knew about what had happened. He sat back on the couch, rubbing his lips and chin with his fingers, unsure of where to begin. He finally decided just to cut to the chase.

"I got her pregnant."

Stratton's neck jerked forward, and he straightened his glasses. "What? What the hell, Fitz? *You did what*?"

Fitz shook his head, biting his bottom lip. His voice was low and throaty when he continued. "It was an accident. We used a condom, but she was a virgin and we sort of started, then stopped and started again, and then finally, you know . . . and it broke."

"Jesus, Fitz." Stratton looked at Fitz thoughtfully. "Pregnant. You said you were about to turn twenty, right? You went to England at the end of that summer. She got pregnant, and you went to England?"

"We didn't know if she was pregnant or not. She went home the next day."

"Oh," said Stratton, sighing heavily. "Then what?"

"Well, I proposed. The morning she left I asked her to marry me, just in case."

"What? *You did what*?" Stratton asked for the second time, eyes bugging out of his head.

"I asked her to marry me. Gave her my high school ring to make it official."

"And she said yes."

Fitz swallowed, remembering her puffy, frightened eyes as she'd taken the ring and slipped it on her finger.

"She did," Fitz whispered, wincing at the memory.

"You know? I would've believed this story from Weston or Barrett. I would've *expected* it of Alex. But *you*?" Stratton shook his head back and forth in shock, adjusting his glasses. "Well, what happened then?"

"Remember when I was home that fall? Right around Columbus Day? Just for a night out of the blue?"

"Yeah. You came home from London for a weekend. Mom said it was a special visit."

"Daisy was in a car accident coming home from school on a Friday afternoon. She called me in London, and I hopped on the first plane to Newark and came home. Went right to the hospital. She miscarried."

"Oh. Oh, man. I had no idea, Fitz. Jesus. I'm sorry."

Fitz swallowed the lump in his throat, nodding at Stratton. "I went back to see her again right before my flight left for London on Sunday. I told her to keep the ring, that I'd still marry her anyway."

"And?"

"And she threw the ring at my head, said that she hated me and I'd ruined her life, and I should go the hell back to London and never bother her again."

"So you did."

"So I did," he whispered, the terrible memories making him feel sick to his stomach. He suddenly remembered he hadn't eaten anything all night. "Got anything to eat, Strat?"

"I'll order pizza. Hang tight."

Stratton took out his cell to order food, and Fitz unbuttoned another button in his shirt and finished the rest of his beer. It felt both good and awful to replay the events of that fall. Good to remember how much he had loved Daisy. Awful to remember her angry eyes and tear-streaked face when she told him to get lost.

"Then what?" asked Stratton softly, returning to sit down.

"Then nothing. A few months later, on Boxing Day, I asked Emily how she was doing, and she told me that Daisy had moved out to California to live with her mother. She was gone. Just like that."

"You never reached out to her? Never called or wrote to her or anything?"

"I wanted to. But I forced myself not to. I got her pregnant, Strat. She was seventeen and she trusted me and I got her pregnant, and then, God, she lost the baby. If she never wanted to see me again, the least I could do was honor her wishes."

"Wow," said Stratton, leaning back in his chair, staring at Fitz with compassion.

"If she'd ever written to me . . . ever called . . . ever needed anything, I would've dropped everything, anything, to help her, to see her, to . . ."

"Hey," said Stratton thoughtfully. "You didn't mean to hurt her. You were really just a kid too."

"No. No, I wasn't. I was twenty. She was a teenager. I knew better than to get involved with her, but there was something about her." *There's* still *something about her.* Fitz shook his head back and forth, feeling miserable. "She was so beautiful and young and fun. Everything was a game. Everything was exciting with Daisy. I'd never known anyone like her before—all the girls in Haverford were so, I don't know, like sisters or something. I'd known them my whole life. She was like a runaway train, and I just wanted to hitch a ride, and . . . I don't know how to explain it, but I felt more alive that summer than I'd ever felt before." *Or since,* he thought sadly. "There were no rules. There was just Daisy." He looked at his brother, horrified to feel a burn at the backs of his eyes. "And then she was gone."

Stratton sipped his beer in respectful silence as Fitz's words sank in. "So what happened tonight?" he finally asked.

"I walked into the Hotel du Pont, and there she was: Daisy Edwards in the flesh after nine years. And she was standing there with her . . . her *goddamn* fiancé. And he was *such* an *asshole* to her, I ended up punching him in the face. Possibly broke his nose." He shrugged. "I don't know. Daisy was furious. Called me a Neanderthal. I didn't stay to find out if he was okay."

Stratton handed Fitz another beer, which Fitz took by rote and threw back. It was starting to do its work. He was mellowing out a little.

Stratton didn't say anything immediately, and when Fitz looked up, his younger brother was desperately trying not to laugh and losing the battle. "You beat up your ex-girlfriend's boyfriend."

"Technically her fiancé."

Stratton snickered quietly, his shoulders quaking as he stared down at the floor. "Jesus, Fitz."

Fitz shook his head back and forth, leaning forward on his knees as he felt his own laughter start. He laughed until the waiting tears filled his eyes and his belly ached. "Oh, man. I haven't seen her in nine years, and the first thing I do is beat up her boyfriend. Jeez."

Stratton sat back in his chair, finishing off his beer and putting the empty bottle on the shiny hardwood floor. "So what next?"

"Hell if I know," said Fitz, then quieter. "She's moving back here."

"Is that good or bad?" asked Stratton.

"Honestly, I don't know." He rubbed his forehead, thinking of what she was about to say to her fiancé just before Fitz hit him. She was about to say that they were just "old friends." Except he'd *never* felt that way about Daisy, and even after all this time, *friends* rang hollow. He didn't want to be her friend. He wanted to be her everything, and he definitely wanted her in his bed. "Bad."

"You still care about her."

"Yeah," said Fitz softly without a second thought. "I never got over her."

Stratton nodded sagely. "You and Barrett and these Edwards girls."

"Just thank God there weren't three more, Strat, or you, Alex, and Wes would be down for the count too."

"There's a pretty big problem, though," said Stratton. "She's getting married, Fitz."

"I heard," said Fitz bitterly.

The doorbell rang, alerting them to pizza, and Stratton hopped up to answer it while Fitz slumped back down into the couch, opening another beer. He remembered the way Dr. M. had manhandled and intimidated her, and his eyes narrowed.

She's not getting married to him, thought Fitz, telling himself he'd do whatever he had to to help her see that Dr. M. was no good for her. *She didn't want to marry me? Fine. But she's not marrying him. Over my dead body.*

Chapter 3

Daisy woke up in the two-bedroom suite she'd reserved at the Hotel du Pont, got out of bed, and peeked into the sitting room to see if Josh was up yet. Didn't look like it. No wonder. It was eight o'clock here, but only five in the morning for her and Josh. While she was an early riser, baking at the crack of dawn, Josh probably wouldn't be up for hours.

She changed into workout clothes and slipped out of the suite quietly to use the fitness center. At home she had a stationary bike, and although she didn't love working out, no one who baked cookies for a living could skimp on the exercise. If she did, she'd be as fat as a house in a month.

She pressed the elevator button, praying that she didn't run into her cousin, who was staying here with Barrett, or any of the other Englishes or Edwardses, though she was fairly sure the rest of them had headed back to Philly after the gala last night. For her part, she'd spent the remainder of the night in her suite with an irate Josh, convincing him not to file assault charges against Fitz and persuading him to stay the night and not take the red-eye back to Portland.

Her head was still spinning over last night.

She swiped her card against the card reader and was relieved to find the fitness center mostly empty. Two middle-aged women walked next to each other on treadmills, chatting, and a younger man kept a good pace on the third of four treadmills. He winked at her when she entered, but she pretended not to notice and headed for the bikes.

She started slowly, grateful for the time to figure out what the hell had happened last night. Illumination came pretty easy.

Despite the surprising strength of Daisy's feelings for Fitz and her panty-sopping attraction to him, everything had happened within the bounds of expectations last night . . . until the end.

She reviewed everything carefully.

She'd expected their reunion to be awkward, and it was in some ways. Though, to be honest, she hadn't expected it to be so charged. She'd sort of assumed that Fitz had forgotten her over the years and that, while she'd have to fight against the power of her attraction to him, he'd be more or less indifferent to her.

She could tell he'd been thrown off by seeing her, and their first attempts at conversation were stilted and uncomfortable, but they'd eventually segued from polite pleasantries into an old rhythm of easy banter. And for a few minutes, she'd thought maybe they could leave the past behind and move forward as friendly acquaintances who shared a brief and ancient history.

What had truly surprised her were two things:

First, Daisy was almost positive that their attraction to each other was both instantaneous and entirely mutual.

She remembered the way he looked at her, his eyes raking down her body, undressing her, when they were first reunited. That same heat in his gaze, hot and unsatisfied, had flared up several more times throughout the evening. The way his breath caught when their hands touched. His lips brushing against her cheek. The way he flipped his hand over to lace his fingers through hers. She couldn't deny it. After all this time, he was still attracted to her.

Daisy had underestimated him. She'd underestimated herself. But more than anything, she'd underestimated their chemistry together.

She quickened her pace on the bike, droplets of sweat dripping down her face.

The second, far more confusing surprise was how emotional Fitz had been with her—the anger in his eyes when he'd mentioned their brief engagement, his eager chuckle as she teased him about his boring deals, and the way his face had softened when she'd reached for his hand. She'd expected polite indifference from him; what she'd seen—before Josh's inopportune interruption—was genuine emotion, vibrant feelings that weren't latent holdovers from nine years ago, but alive and urgent. And after Josh's interruption? Hitting him like a jealous, protective boyfriend? She couldn't have been more shocked. What in the world did it mean?

None of this was part of her plan, and yet she might be seeing the answer to a question that had always haunted her. They'd had such an effortlessly good time together that summer—without the complication of pregnancy, would they would have parted ways and maybe found each other again down the line? Between their compatibility and attraction, would they have had a chance? *Maybe,* she thought. *We might have.*

The broken condom had complicated things. Fitz had asked her to marry him only because he feared she was pregnant. He'd *never* told her that he loved her, not the night they'd made love; not the next morning, when he proposed; not in his mostly sterile letters to her from London that were concerned about her health; not even when she was lying in a hospital bed, having broken her leg and several ribs and miscarried his child. And while she knew he had cared for her on *some* level, without the word *love*, despite ample opportunity, she'd come to believe that the summer they'd spent together was just a fling. Or it would have been, had responsibility and guilt not entered the equation the second the condom broke.

I'd do anything for you.

The words resonated in her head, making her wince. She knew that Fitz would do anything to settle the debt between them. She'd known it when he offered her his high school ring as an engagement ring the morning after their tryst. She'd known it again when he arrived at the hospital straight from London. She'd known it before he said good-bye, when he told her, "I'll still marry you," despite her miscarriage. Knowing his motive was honor, not love, Daisy had thrown his ring at his head, telling him she didn't need his pity or his stupid ring, and he should go back to London and never, ever bother her for as long as she lived. In a strange way, she even knew that he hadn't contacted her for all these years because she'd told him to leave her alone so definitively. It was his way of honoring her wishes.

But now they'd been reunited, and amid scorching attraction and uncharacteristically indiscriminate emotion, his guilt was the least confusing thing about last night and the one thing Daisy felt she could address.

I'd do anything for you.

Even now, nine years later, he still perceived there was a debt to settle.

She needed for him to understand that he was wrong. If there ever *had* been a debt between them, which was arguable in the first place, since she had wanted him just as badly that night by the pool as he had wanted her, it had been forgiven long ago. The sheer force of her love for him hadn't allowed her to hold a grudge. All she wanted for Fitz was a happy and full life loving someone as much as Daisy had once loved him. She wanted him to have the chance to find that sort of happiness, unencumbered by the weight of the past. Her heart insisted that she gift him his freedom from any misguided sense of obligation, and that's exactly what she intended to do. Getting over Fitz emotionally was her problem, not his, but by setting him free, she hoped it would set her free too.

Circling back to their attraction and his unexpected emotions, she broke into a sweat that had nothing to do with her workout.

If she intended to hold on to her sanity, being with Fitz physically simply wasn't an option. Though she'd never been Miss Right for Fitz English, if the heat in his eyes told her anything, it assured her that Miss Right Now was up for grabs. But despite her loneliness, Daisy wasn't interested in being *anyone's* Miss Right Now. Not even Fitz English's.

Her body protested this decision as she remembered the feeling of his lips against her cheek, the heat of his hand laced through hers.

She told her body to shut the hell up.

First of all, she was still technically "engaged" in the eyes of her friends and family, and Daisy wasn't a cheater, so until she and Dr. M. officially "broke up" she simply wasn't available to be Fitz English's plaything.

And second of all, she had more maturity and self-respect than would allow her to engage in a purely physical fling with someone who didn't genuinely care for her. Daisy was lonely, but in an encouraging burst of spirit, she realized that she wasn't desperate. She wanted wedding rings and a home and children. She wanted deep, mutual, unconditional love. She wanted someone to be so crazy about her that nothing and no one would get in the way of him having her.

She sighed, wishing that life had turned out differently for them. But she also saw things clearly. There was only a past for her and Fitz to reconcile, not a future to look forward to. The sooner Fitz let go of his obligation to her, the sooner Daisy could let go of her love for him, and the sooner they could both get on with their lives. And after nine years of his guilt and her unrequited love, the only wish-come-true they both deserved was the freedom to finally move on.

Fitz's mouth felt as dry as cotton balls, and his head thumped with the drums of a hundred high school marching bands. He opened his eyes slowly, the effort painful, trying to orient himself. Blinking twice, he tried to lean up, but his cheek clung to the surface beneath him. He jerked his neck a little and dislodged himself from dried saliva and black leather, but the effort made his head start pounding all over again. He leaned on his elbows, looking around at Stratton's living room as the details of last night started careening back toward him.

The Hotel du Pont . . . Daisy Edwards . . . asshole fiancé . . . bloody nose . . . Strat . . . beer . . . pizza . . . beer, beer, beer.

He sat up, wincing from the throbbing in his head. He looked groggily over at the kitchen, from which the smell of coffee wafted— pretty much the only smell on the face of the earth that wouldn't make him want to heave.

"Feeling like total crap, brother of mine?" asked Stratton with a grin.

A mug was plunked down on the coffee table before him, and Fitz stared at it for a second before bringing it to his mouth, the bitter goodness clearing out the cotton balls and soothing his aching throat.

"I've felt better." Fitz scratched his stubbly jaw, looking around for his phone.

"I took it away. You said you were going to call every Daisy Edwards in Greater Philadelphia."

"She's probably not even listed yet."

Stratton rolled his eyes. "The sort of logic that didn't work on you last night."

"Sorry, Strat," said Fitz sheepishly.

His younger brother straightened his glasses and reached into his sweatshirt pocket for a little container of Advil. He shook it lightly before opening it. "I recommend four."

Fitz nodded weakly, taking the tablets gratefully and washing them down with more hot coffee.

"Alex should be here in"—Stratton looked at his watch—"about twenty minutes."

"Oh, yeah? He doesn't have some brunette to take to brunch?"

"My guess is that the brunette *and* the redhead he entertained last night are taking each other out to brunch . . . since you insisted that he get his ass over here by ten or you wouldn't be brothers anymore."

Fitz winced. "Was that right around the time you took my phone away?"

Stratton pursed his lips and nodded. "Seemed like the right move."

"Did I happen to mention to Alex why I required his presence in my life at ten o'clock on a Sunday morning?"

"You did, in fact. Alex is supposed to run some quick numbers and approve a loan. I am supposed to find a building suitable for use as a café in Haverford. And you are supposed to finalize the contracts."

"What contracts?"

"Real estate, small business, and articles of incorporation. For Daisy's Delights."

"Ohhhhhh, Jesus."

It was happening again. That reckless thing that happened when he found himself anywhere in the vicinity of Daisy Edwards. Hitting people. Getting drunk. Wild schemes to start businesses without the permission of the proprietor.

"Yeah. And I'd tell you it was all just the harmless ramblings of a drunkard, but while I was taking the pizza box and the first of your six empties to the incinerator, you somehow managed to write a coherent twelve-line press release, which you sent to the *Philadelphia Sun*, informing them that Daisy's Delights, the premier bakery of Portland, Oregon, was opening a branch in Haverford, Pennsylvania, in six weeks."

"Six weeks?"

"Yeah. You're aiming for December and the Christmas traffic, apparently. Thank God you didn't say six days."

Fitz took a deep breath, feeling sick. Although he remembered Daisy mentioning a sort of vague plan to one day open a bakery, he'd had absolutely no right to take matters into his own hands. *What had he been thinking?* Short answer: he hadn't. He was blinded to logic because he wasn't lying last night when he said he'd do anything for her. But this was ridiculous and would just have to be undone.

"I'll cancel it. The press release. You can call Alex and tell him to go another round with the brunette and the redhead. I'm sure he'll be grateful."

Stratton reached beside his chair and picked up the newspaper. "Too late, I'm afraid. You gave them the number of your Platinum Amex and told them not to worry about the cost but to give you prime placement in the Sunday edition." Stratton held up the first page of the Lifestyles section, where a full-column article, including Daisy's picture, indicated in bold letters, "Daisy's Delights: Coming Soon to Soothe Your Sweet Tooth!"

"Oh my God. You have *got* to be kidding me." Fitz grabbed for the paper, staring at the article in disbelief. His name . . . his family's company . . . Daisy's name . . . bakery, great coffee, Haverford. It was all there. Her picture. The logo from her website. "Jesus, Strat. Where the hell's your incinerator?! Were you gone for four hours?"

"I got to talking to the girl down the hall. Her ex-boyfriend plays games with her head. She needed to vent."

"Friend-zoned by the girl down the hall," snorted Fitz.

"Friends is comfortable."

"Try the flip side. It's delicious."

"This from you? You're in the middle of the biggest debacle of your life because of your schlong. You know it and I know it. You've got it bad for this girl, and it's ruining your judgment."

Stratton was right. He was one hundred percent right.

"This is a disaster. This is a goddamned disaster," Fitz moaned, shaking his head back and forth disbelievingly at the newspaper, the growing lump in his throat compounded by the swirling in his stomach.

Just go the hell back to London! Can't you see you've ruined my life? Leave me alone. Don't ever, ever bother me again.

The words came rushing back as though she'd said them yesterday, and he winced, closing his eyes as a bead of sweat worked its way down his face. Yet again he tried to fix things for the woman he loved. Yet again she was going to hate him for it.

"What am I going to do?" groaned Fitz, holding his head in his hands.

"You're going to call Barrett, explain fast, and tell him to take Daisy and her fiancé out for a nice long breakfast so she doesn't see the morning paper. I already found two suitable places for commercial rent in Haverford village. I also spent a few hours this morning researching what it costs to start a café, so I've got some ballpark numbers for Alex. When he gets here, we're going to draw up the loan for Daisy. You'll take a shower while I find a real estate agent willing to show us the two spaces, and then we'll drive out to Haverford. Mom'll be delighted to see us for Sunday supper, you know."

This was textbook Stratton. Fixing everything for someone he loved. It's what he did. And Fitz had never felt more grateful for him.

"But Fitz. What are you going to do about Daisy? I'm going to make sure I'm not in throwing range when you tell her what you've been up to. Just in case she's wearing a ring. Maybe we should stop and get you a helmet too," he added as he sauntered to his bedroom to take a shower.

Then again, grateful *may be too strong a word.*

"Well, Dr. M.," said Emily, "we're sorry to hear you're headed back to Portland tonight. We were hoping to have a chance to get to know you a little better."

Daisy had asked Josh just to be himself for the remainder of the trip, and breakfast with Barrett and Emily had gone pretty smoothly, except for the nervous way Barrett kept looking over at her. Did he hold her responsible for Fitz's outrageous behavior last night? Or—oh God, her heart sank—did he know about what had happened between her and Fitz years ago? Maybe he was judging her? She'd always just assumed Fitz would have protected her by keeping their sordid history to himself, but what if Barrett knew?

"To be honest, Emily, I'll be glad to get home. Not sure if Philly's for me."

Daisy whipped her eyes to Josh—they'd agreed that he'd still play her fiancé for the remainder of the day. She shot him a frantic, beseeching look.

"B-but, I'll try to love it . . . for Daisy."

Daisy's shoulders relaxed, and she gave Josh a weak smile.

"You said one of your patients needs an emergency surgery tomorrow?" asked Barrett.

"I'm afraid so," answered Josh. "Abscess. From the pictures, it looks like a mess. I'll take the red-eye and operate first thing in the morning."

"Without a good night's sleep?" asked Emily.

"Oh, J—Mel can sleep on the plane, right, honey?"

"I'll sure try."

Emily raised an eyebrow, then turned her no-nonsense glare to Daisy. "Can I speak to you for a moment? Outside?"

Daisy gave Josh and Barrett a tight smile before following Emily out of the café and onto the sidewalk.

"What the heck is going on?"

Daisy shrugged. "What do you mean?"

"Your fiancé is suddenly returning to Portland. He clearly doesn't like Philly, and there's no way he can operate on someone after a red-eye, so that's got to be a lie. Is he—are you two breaking up, Daisy? Be honest. I can tell something's not right."

She didn't have much of a choice, but at least she could swear Emily to secrecy. Not only that, but it would be a relief not to have to pretend around someone.

"It's not going to work out," said Daisy, shrugging. "Mel's heading back to Portland for good, and I'm staying here."

Emily's face contorted in sympathy, and she opened her arms to Daisy, making Daisy's guilt quadruple. "Oh, Daze. I'm so sorry!"

She patted Emily's back awkwardly as Emily held her close.

"It's, um, it's okay, Em. We've been, um, growing apart for a . . . a while now? Yeah. And so . . . you know, I'm okay. He'll be happy there, and I'll just, you know, make a fresh start here."

Emily leaned back, putting her hands on Daisy's shoulders. "You're so strong. I'd be a mess if I lost Barrett."

Daisy almost laughed. Comparing her sham engagement to the genuine, once-in-a-lifetime passion shared between her cousin and Barrett English was outlandish. She might have laughed if her jealousy hadn't kicked in.

"Then you should probably snap him up."

Emily grimaced. "Fitz sort of wrecked that for me last night."

Daisy's eyes widened, and her mouth dropped. "You were going to—"

Emily nodded. "Last night. I was going to put the ring on as we danced after dinner. But then Fitz hit Mel, and we had to help you two, and by the time we returned to the ball, they'd cleared dinner and I was starving, so we ended up sneaking out to McDonald's and I couldn't bear to put on my engagement ring over a Big Mac."

"Oh, Em. I'm so sorry."

"I'll find an even better moment. Maybe even tonight. You're coming to Sunday supper, aren't you? After you drop off Dr. M. at the airport?"

"Sunday supper?" Daisy asked weakly.

"At Haverford Park. Ever since Barrett and I started dating, we've all gotten together every Sunday evening at five o'clock. Eleanora always had a Sunday supper, and so did my mom. It seemed silly to me and Barrett for us to have separate dinners a five-minute walk away, so we convinced the moms to combine efforts in exchange for attending every week. So far, so good."

"It's not . . . awkward?"

Emily shrugged, a smile creeping up the corners of her mouth. "You know Eleanora. She somehow makes things happen."

"Anyway," continued Emily, "as long as you're staying at the gatehouse with Mom and Dad until you find your own place, it would only be awkward if you *didn't* come."

"Does my dad go?"

"Of course!" said Emily. "It's been nice to have him around more. I know it means a lot to my dad to have his brother a little closer."

"Then I guess I'll be there."

And Daisy's stupid heart leaped because maybe Fitz would be there too. *Oh God, please let him—don't let him—let him—don't let him be there.*

Emily noticed the conflict on her cousin's face and pulled her into another embrace. "Oh, Daze, here I am going on about Barrett and engagements and family dinners while your heart is probably in shambles. I'm so sorry."

"Really, Em. It's fine. Like I said, Mel and I have been more and more distant lately. He never even got me a ring. It's probably for the best." She leaned back and looked into her cousin's eyes, so much like her own. "But do me a favor? Don't tell anyone. Not yet. Not your folks. Not my dad. Not even Barrett. It's, um, it's so embarrassing. Let me tell everyone in my own time, okay?"

"I understand," said Emily, pretending to lock her lips and throw away the key. "Mum's the word. You're very strong."

I hope so, thought Daisy, following Emily back into the café to finish brunch before packing up and driving Josh to the airport for his late-afternoon check-in. *Because it's going to take all the strength I have to push gorgeous, complicated Fitz English out of my heart.*

Chapter 4

As Fitz drove himself and Stratton through the gates of Haverford Park that evening, he was finally starting to feel better about everything.

Earlier that day, Alex, who had arrived at Stratton's in his tux from last night, smelling like a brothel, had arranged a loan for Daisy from English & Sons and left Fitz with a check for a hundred and twenty grand in her name.

Alex never directly asked why Fitz needed this done, though his knowing smirk said plenty, and he'd departed with the sage advice: "This time, maybe you should actually tell her how you feel about her."

"What's that supposed to mean?"

"That summer? Everyone, and I mean *everyone*, knew how you felt . . . except her. She always had that uncertain look in her eyes, searching your face from across the room, across the pool deck, across the tennis courts, like she was wondering where she ranked in your life."

"You don't know what you're talking about." He thought about going to the hospital the second time, despite his mother's warnings, how he'd told her he still wanted to marry her. What had her response been? He winced inwardly, recalling the way his ring had pinged off his forehead. "Just because you sleep with a lot of women, Alex, doesn't mean you understand them."

"Uh, actually, yeah. It sort of does. Not to mention, I was there all summer with a front row seat to all your shenanigans. I followed you two around in the dark more than once too."

"What the hell?" Fitz cringed, uncomfortable knowing, all these years later, that his private moments with Daisy had been invaded by his younger brother. "You're disgusting."

"That is true. But I was a horny nineteen-year-old, and she was the hottest thing I'd ever seen. Not that she ever even noticed me. I could pretty much nail any tail in Haverford, but Daisy Edwards only had eyes for you."

"Yeah, well, it didn't last. It was just a summer thing."

"Seemed more serious than that," said Alex softly, and Fitz narrowed his eyes. Did Alex know? About the pregnancy? Fitz stared into Alex's face, and Alex colored slightly, dropping Fitz's eyes. Damn it, he knew.

Fitz bristled, feeling exposed and annoyed. "In case you didn't notice, she's getting married, Alex. We're finished talking about this."

"She's not married *yet*," Alex said calmly. "Whatever happened between you two? She was into you in a big way. From where I was sitting, it looked like she was in love with you."

"If I have to tell you to shut up again," said Fitz in a level voice, cracking his knuckles before putting his hands on his hips, "I'm going to deck you."

Alex shook his head at Fitz like he was a lost cause, handing him the check for Daisy. "Listen, I know she's engaged, but she's here, and if you still care about her . . . Jesus, if you still love her . . ." He paused, clenching his jaw, looking uncharacteristically bothered for a moment. "Not everyone gets a second chance, Fitz. This is yours. Don't blow it."

He watched Alex saunter out the door casually, with his tux jacket slung over his shoulder, feeling his chest tighten from the impact of his brother's words.

Was it true? Did Daisy not know how Fitz had felt about her that summer?

They'd spent every minute together. They'd had sex. He'd asked her to marry him. Those weren't the ambiguous actions of a man who didn't care about a woman. He wasn't given to fancy words and flowery sentiment—he never had been. It wasn't Fitz's way. He was more comfortable showing how he felt than he was putting his feelings into words. Surely Daisy had known how he felt that summer. It was written in every smile, every look, every time he touched her or kissed her, how crazy he was about her. She had to have known—on some level, whether she returned his feelings or not—how much he loved her, indeed how deeply in love with her he'd been.

But she was young and carefree. She'd just wanted a fling—a casual summer thing that ended in losing her virginity. Because up until the moment the condom broke, everything had been pretty much perfect. In fact, several times that night Fitz had almost told her that he loved her, but swallowed the words because he didn't want to bring a heaviness to the fun, lighthearted nature of their relationship. And he certainly didn't want to pressure her into saying the words back. He told himself that it was okay to hold on to them until the time was right. It was okay to bide his time.

In fact, he'd even convinced himself that it was okay if she didn't love him as much as he loved her. For starters, she was younger than he was. And she needed to finish high school, and he needed to go to London and finish college. Fitz had taken a long, realistic, and rational view of their relationship. She'd always be in his sphere of influence, returning to visit Emily and her parents. He'd look forward to those moments, and someday they'd both be adults, mature enough for love and commitment. When that day came along, Fitz would make his move after quietly loving her for years. When that day came along, he'd ask her to be his wife.

But then he'd gotten her pregnant and blew the whole plan to hell. At the time, he decided she was probably confused and worried enough without him pushing her emotionally to return feelings she might or might not have for him. They had to deal with the situation of her possible, then actual, pregnancy. He purposely kept his letters from England unemotional, desperate that she never feel pressured into loving him just because he loved her, desperate to give her the space to decide what she wanted to do about the baby, and in his heart he committed to being there for her, no matter what she decided to do.

Hadn't she seen that? He would have done anything for her. Married her and had the baby. Supported her decision not to have it or give it up for adoption. Throwing his feelings into the mix would have been selfish, would have just confused things. And a seventeen-year-old girl expecting a baby doesn't require further confusion.

Especially from the person who let her down. It was his condom. He was the more experienced of them. He was the almost adult while she was still a teen. But when she whispered, "This is all we have left," it blasted any good judgment out of the water. Faced with a life without Daisy for at least a year while he was in London? It was so bleak and disheartening, he lost himself in her instead. He took everything she offered him. Her body. Her virginity. Her innocence. Her home. She'd lost so much. And he'd lost nothing . . . except her.

On a good day, Daisy Edwards made him careless. But add his guilt over everything she'd surrendered to him? It blinded him. When he said he'd do anything for her last night, he meant it. Anything. Buy her a bakery. Watch her marry someone else who made her happy.

Anything. He'd apologize to her and Dr. M. the next time he saw
them. He had no business trying to mess up her future. Luckily, he
and Stratton had found a perfect space for Daisy's Delights in bus-
tling Haverford village, only ten minutes from Haverford Park. He'd
offer the bakery as a peace offering, and then—despite the whisper-
ings of his heart and longings of his flesh—he'd leave her alone, just
as she'd asked him to so many years ago.

As Daisy walked up the gravel driveway, toward the great house, with
Emily and her father, aunt, and uncle, her heart thumped with anticipation. Would Fitz be here tonight? Without wanting to seem obvious, she'd asked Emily at breakfast which of the brothers showed up
regularly for dinner, but Emily answered that it changed every week,
depending on who was around and available. Sometimes it was just
her and Barrett; other times, all four younger brothers managed to
show up at the same time. Emily grinned, sharing that those dinners
were always the most fun.

Josh had looked very relieved to say good-bye at the airport, insist-
ing Daisy not go to the trouble of parking and walking in with him.
He turned to her just before getting out of the car.

"I'm not one to butt into people's personal affairs, but are you sure
you're going to be okay?"

She nodded. "I think so."

"You never told me exactly why you needed a fake fiancé, Daisy,
but you clearly have unfinished business with that guy, Fitz. Can't say
I like him, but I hope you get it sorted out."

"Me too, Josh," she said, giving him a small smile. "And sorry,
again, for what happened."

Josh waved away her apology, continuing, "Probably best to lay
your cards on the table, you know? Don't assume he knows what
you're thinking. When I get home, I'm asking Sara Meyers out on a
date. I'm going to tell her I've been in like with her for about three
years now. And well now, maybe she won't like that, or maybe she will.
But, it's better than wondering." He leaned over and kissed her cheek.
"Good-bye, Stella. Good luck."

Daisy turned this over in her head as she and her family walked
by the carefully trimmed hedges that her uncle kept meticulously
maintained on the grand driveway. Unfinished business? Yes. What
kind? Damned if she knew. So much between her and Fitz seemed
unsaid.

Emily linked her arm through Daisy's as the gravel crunched under their feet. "Remember that night on the trampoline? The night Fitz stole the wine and we all got drunk?"

Daisy grinned. "I remember."

"Barrett walked us home that night."

"Yes, he did. I remember."

"I don't. I must have been three sheets to the wind."

"You were."

"You know," said Emily conspiratorially, "I sort of thought that you and Fitz had a thing going on that summer."

"Did you?"

"Uh-huh. I mean, I never saw you guys making out or anything, but you were always staring at each other. It seemed . . . intense."

Daisy was quiet, even though Emily was fishing. By tacit agreement, she and Fitz had kept their relationship a secret—partially because there were a lot of personalities in play that summer, but mostly because sneaking around was part of the fun. It had heightened the excitement of their time together, and she'd loved it.

"And you know," continued Emily, "he's single. He dates a lot, but—"

"But what?" demanded Daisy without thinking.

Emily looked at Daisy thoughtfully and shrugged. "He never seems to stay with anyone for more than a couple of months, but maybe things would be different for you . . . Once you get over Dr. M., you could always cast your eyes his way."

"Fitz's way?"

"Yep. And I know he might seem sort of boring—"

"Boring?" exclaimed Daisy defensively. "He's *not* boring."

"I just mean he's very reserved."

"Oh yes. Punching strangers in the face is very reserved, Emmy."

"I don't know what happened last night," said Emily. "I couldn't have been more shocked! Barrett tells me all the time that Fitz is the most ethical person he knows. They'll never owe a dime to the IRS or the FCC, because Fitz follows every rule, every law to the letter. I can't imagine what happened to make him behave like that."

"Dr. M. made an off-color joke," Daisy covered quickly. "I pretended to be insulted, and Fitz took it the wrong way."

"Like I said. There was always something very intense between you two."

"It was a million years ago. Besides, I'm still 'engaged,' right?"

Emily sighed. "I guess. Though it would be fun to be cousins *and* sisters-in-law, wouldn't it?"

"Emily!" exclaimed Daisy, breaking into giggles. "You haven't even said yes yet!"

Daisy was so distracted by her cousin, she missed the sight of Fitz and Stratton coming around the house from the garage, so she was surprised when she heard Fitz call her name just as his mother opened the massive front door to welcome them.

"Daisy!"

Her heart immediately started galloping, and Daisy dropped Emily's arm, turning to face Fitz as the rest of her family was ushered inside by Mrs. English.

He approached her across the gravel, stopping a few feet away, as Stratton covered his head with his hands and hurried ahead of Fitz into the house.

"Can I talk to you?"

He was wearing ironed khaki pants and a light blue gingham shirt rolled up to the elbows. The hair on the back of his neck brushed his collar. His blond hair was darker now than it had been nine years ago, almost more like a light brown streaked with gold, but still wavy and tousled. Her fingers twitched, remembering how it felt.

"Sure," she said, turning to look at Mrs. English apologetically.

"Mom, Daisy and I are going to take a walk before dinner."

"Don't be long," said his mother, giving Daisy a thin smile before returning to her guests.

They fell into an easy rhythm, turning toward the gardens that led down a hill to the tennis courts, Fitz walking beside her with his hands shoved into his pants pockets.

"I'm sorry," he finally said after they'd been walking in silence for a few minutes, "about last night. I was hoping that Dr. M. would join us this evening so I could apologize to him as well."

"He had to go back to Portland."

"What?" asked Fitz, putting a hand on her arm and stopping their walk. Was that a flicker of hope in his eyes?

"An emergency surgery."

"But he'll be back soon?"

Daisy shook her head and started walking again. When Fitz caught up with her, he walked closer to her than he had before and his arm brushed with hers.

"No. I'm . . ." She cleared her throat nervously. "I'm afraid he won't be back immediately. He has several more appointments over the next few weeks that he feels obligated to take care of."

"What are you saying? He's staying in Portland without you?"

"Temporarily," she said, hoping lightning wouldn't strike her dead for lying.

"That doesn't bother you?"

His arm brushed into hers with every step, and it felt so good she didn't move away. She let it brush into hers over and over again, pretending she didn't notice. Did he notice too? Did it affect him as much as it did her? Did he savor the contact as she did?

"Did you want to talk to me about something?"

"Well, I wanted to say I was sorry for hitting your fiancé. That was unacceptable."

"Agreed."

"But I did *not* like the way he spoke to you."

"It's none of your business, Fitz," she whispered, realizing that they'd changed course at some point, crossing the back lawn so that they weren't headed toward the tennis courts anymore. They were headed toward the pool. She inhaled raggedly, pulling her upper lip between her teeth. She looked back at the house, knowing she should turn and head up the hill to their waiting families, but the truth was, she treasured these moments alone with Fitz. She didn't want to go back yet.

"Are you happy?" he asked quietly.

She swallowed. "Does it matter?"

"To me, it does."

Her heart caught, the old impulse to look beyond the words to find meaning behind them making her breathless for a moment.

"Why?"

"We're almost at the pool," he observed offhandedly, his arm brushing hers again.

"Why, Fitz? Why does it matter to you if I'm happy?"

She didn't know what she was doing. She had no business opening this can of worms. She was supposed to be engaged. But maybe that's what gave her the courage. From outward appearances, she had no designs on him. It made her feel safer.

At the split rail fence that surrounded the pool, Fitz rested his elbows, looking at the dark green plastic cover over the rectangular pool. Pool chairs were neatly lined up in the corner of the deck, waiting for sunny days to arrive again. The sun was getting lower in the sky, and the deep, honey light bounced off his hair, making it look like woven gold.

"Because I took happiness away from you," he said softly. "Because you trusted me and I let you down. Because you deserve to be happy."

He was trying to be kind, but his words hurt her. She wanted him to say "Because I loved you then, and I love you now, and the only way we can be happy is if we're together." Sadly, his words had voiced only his regret and his responsibility to her. But the burst of pain somehow made her feel stronger and more determined. She looked down at the rough-hewn rails—at her small, very white fingers next to his tan arm that was lightly sprinkled with coarse blond hair. Inside her chest, her heart had so much love for him that it twisted with sadness, but her mind was clear.

"I'm happy enough," she answered curtly. "You don't need to worry."

He turned his head as she looked at him, and it occurred to her that they were lined up perfectly to kiss. All he'd need to do is drop his lips and they'd fall on hers. She stared at his mouth for a long moment, remembering the firmness and softness of his kiss, the way he moved his lips over hers insistently, hungrily. When she looked back to his eyes, there was almost no blue left except for thin rings of aqua around pools of obsidian. Her chest heaved from the heaviness of her breathing, and she dropped her gaze quickly to his lips, then back to his eyes, begging him to do something that they both knew he shouldn't do.

Her upturned face was so sad when she said *happy enough* that he didn't believe her, and despite her reassurance, he *was* worried. But he'd forgotten about everything—their conversation, the bakery he needed to tell her about, his apology, her happiness—when she'd trained her eyes on his lips and lingered there. She stared at him like she was remembering every time he'd pressed his mouth to hers, every time his tongue had claimed hers, sucking and sliding over hers, because he could never, ever get enough of her. His body tightened next to her, leaning against the fence, so close to the pool where she'd given herself to him once upon a time.

Her scumbag fiancé had left her in Philly alone, and right now, right here, Daisy was with him. Standing beside *him*, with her small, perfect breasts straining against her pink scoop-neck shirt. Alex's words came back to him: *Not everyone gets a second chance, Fitz. This is yours.* She had her hair in a braid that sat forward on her shoulder, and he reached out for it, staring at the light crisscrosses of hair. Holding her eyes, his fist closed around the braid, gently tugging so that she leaned closer. He'd barely need to do more than drop his neck and his mouth would fall flush on hers.

She didn't pull away, and her eyes, wide and luminous, didn't warn him to stop. His breathing was so shallow he felt dizzy, the silkiness of her hair in his palm like a talisman, possessing him, urging him forward, telling him to reclaim what had always been his.

And he'd never wanted anything in his life as much as he wanted to kiss Daisy Edwards in that moment, but at the same time, he knew he shouldn't. She was getting married, and Fitz had no right to take anything else away from her, and yet, and yet, and yet . . . He closed his eyes, leaning closer to her, depleted of the energy it would take to fight the all-consuming longing he'd never lost for her.

"Fitz . . ." she sighed in a half sob, her breath hot against his lips.

His hand still held her braid tightly, and he panted, his breath mingling with hers, the space of a hair left between them.

"We can't," she whispered, the sound tortured and throaty.

He froze, holding his breath, opening his eyes to find hers closed tightly before him, her breasts still heaving as she took one ragged breath after another. He unfurled his hand and let her braid fall back, leaning away from her as he swallowed the uncomfortable lump in his throat.

"I'm sorry," he said.

"Fitz," she breathed, opening her tear-brightened eyes as she crossed her arms over her chest. She looked dizzy and uncertain, as though coming out of the throes of a dream. "That summer was perfect . . . I mean, I was . . . no, I think I *am* in—"

"—gaged," he finished. He took a deep, gasping breath, turning away from her. "I know. That summer was a long time ago, and you're engaged now. I don't know what's wrong with me. I'm sorry."

She whimpered softly beside him. "That's not what—"

"No. There's no excuse." He bit his bottom lip, shaking his head. "When I'm with you, all common sense seems to fly out the window. I act foolish, ridiculous."

Her eyes flashed, and her tone had a bite to it. "It would be foolish and ridiculous to kiss me?"

"An engaged woman? Yeah. Not to mention unethical, immoral, and just plain wrong. You're not available." He winced as he said this, wishing like hell it wasn't the case. "It's just hard to forget, you know? You're right. That summer was perfect."

Her shoulders slumped, and she turned back toward the pool. "Mostly."

"Completely."

He felt her gaze on his face, staring, searching. He deliberately kept his eyes trained on the pool because if he looked at her, he wouldn't have had the willpower to stop himself from kissing her.

"We should get back," she finally said. "Your mother will wonder—"

"Last night," he blurted out, "you mentioned something about wanting to start a bakery."

She scoffed lightly, cocking her head to the side as she glanced at him. "Someday. Sure, I guess."

"How about now?"

"*Right now?*" She righted her head to stare at him. "I wouldn't know the first thing about getting started."

"What if I said that the groundwork was done? The loan was approved, the real estate was secured, the contracts for incorporation had been filed, the permits approved. Everything done. All you'd need to do is customize the space and start baking."

Her lips tilted up, and she wetted them, which was so goddamn distracting, he purposely dug his elbows into the fence to ground himself.

"What are you talking about, Fitz?"

Her face was a mix of worry and anticipation, and suddenly he knew what he had to do. He took her hand off the fence, lacing it through his, and pulled her toward the garage.

"Come on. I think it's best if I show you."

Chapter 5

Daisy had no idea where they were going, but as soon as they got into Fitz's car, he took out his phone and called his mother.

"Hello?" Eleanora's smooth voice carried over the Bluetooth speaker.

"Mom? Don't wait for us. We're headed into town."

His car churned up gravel as he sped away from the house.

"Fitzpatrick William English," she said in her mom voice. "The table is already set."

"I'm sorry, Mom. I'll explain later."

After a moment of silence, a dial tone sounded to indicate his mother had hung up. Daisy cringed, turning to look at Fitz, who flicked her a quick, uneasy grin, driving down the long driveway with determination.

Without looking away from the windshield, he asked, "You trust me, Daze?"

Daisy looked askance at him, raising an eyebrow. It had taken so much strength to stop him when they almost kissed at the pool. A split second before his lips touched hers, she reminded herself that this was a man who felt he owed her, who was attracted to her but who'd never loved her, who hadn't contacted her in nine years. And that thought gave her the strength to stop him, though she'd gotten so jacked up in the moment, so turned around and emotional, she almost blurted out that she'd been in love with him that summer, and even now, part of her still loved him. Thank God he stopped her. That declaration would have added a whole new level of inappropriate to the equation. Inappropriate? No, that was the wrong word. *Confusion* was far more accurate.

Daisy was confused. And she was starting to wonder if Fitz was feeling it too.

For so long she'd convinced herself Fitz's feelings for her were limited to a summer fling, followed by a sense of obligation over her pregnancy. That their chemistry was just as potent as ever had surprised her last night, but now she was genuinely starting to question his supposed indifference to her. The past and the present were blurring wildly, and, more and more, she was excluding friendship from the list of possible outcomes between them.

Punching Josh last night had been a grand gesture, and now here they were, headed somewhere that had to do with a bakery, and Daisy suspected another grand gesture was coming. And grand gestures, from her limited experience, were born of love, not obligation.

Then again, he'd been pretty clear at the pool when he asked about her happiness that he still felt as though he'd taken something away from her. He wanted to make that up to her, which sounded less like love and more like obligation.

She caught her reflection in the window—her furrowed brows and pouty lips. Daisy didn't like feeling confused, but she couldn't seem to figure out what was going on. If she allowed herself to believe that he had feelings for her, as both Emily and Josh had implied, that would leave her heart in a precarious position. She'd end up falling for Fitz. Again. And probably getting hurt. Again.

He cleared his throat, taking her silence as her answer to his question. "Okay. Fair enough. You don't have to trust me. But I promise you that what I lack in love I make up for in business."

It was such a silly, offhand remark, and yet Daisy couldn't ever remember Fitz using the word *love* in a romantic context at all. Hearing it took her breath away and made tingles go down her back. Every second she spent with him started to feel more and more like that summer, right down to him impulsively taking her hand and driving her into town without an explanation.

He didn't look at her or say anything else as he drove under the marble and wrought iron gates and turned left onto Blueberry Lane. Leaning forward, he turned on the radio, and a sweet, old-timey ukulele riff came gently through the speakers, making Daisy's eyes close in pleasure for a moment as the familiar, though long-forgotten, words surrounded them.

Sweet pea, apple of my eye,
Don't know when and I don't know why
You're the only reason I keep on coming home.

"This song." She sighed, opening her eyes as a dreamy smile spread across her face.

"This song," he said softly, nodding at its goodness.

"It's heaven, right?"

"You remember, Daisy?"

"I remember," she whispered, looking from the massive, beautiful grounds of Haverford Park out her window to his burnished blond head beside her. "If I didn't know you better, Fitz, I'd almost call this romantic."

"Go ahead and call it romantic," he said softly. "I can't hear this song without thinking about you."

Her heart leaped, but she warned herself not to read into his words. Of course he thought of her; they'd heard it together for the first time at a dive bar in Philly ten years ago, when Amos Lee still sang at open mike nights. Fitz was referring to their past, not the present.

"And you know?" he added, in a thoughtful voice. "I think you know me better than most, Daisy. Most people only see one side of me."

"The buttoned-up side?"

He nodded, turning onto Main Street, as Amos Lee sang on:

Sweet pea, keeper of my soul,
I know sometimes I'm out of control . . .
You're the only reason I keep on coming home.

"But I'm more than that when I'm with you. The night we heard this song? You'd somehow convinced me it was a good idea to borrow my dad's Lamborghini without permission and go to a dive bar in the crappiest part of Philly to hear an obscure singer."

"Tell me it wasn't worth it," she teased, rolling her head to the side to look over at him.

"It was worth it." He glanced over and grinned, but his grin faded as he added, "It was *all* worth it, Daze."

He stopped at the first of three stoplights, took the hand closest to her off the steering wheel, and extended it to her, palm up. Her stomach flipped over as she covered it with hers, palm to palm, forcing herself to look away from the mix of heat and regret in his eyes. *This is all part of reconciling the past*, she told herself weakly. *That's all it is.*

"Where are we going?"

"We're almost there," he said, his fingers squeezing hers gently. "You said you wanted to start a bakery last night. A brick-and-mortar place with cookies, cupcakes, and great coffee." He let go of her hand with a sigh. "You could have it all up and running by the time Dr. M. gets back to Philly."

He pulled into a diagonal parking space and turned to her. "We're here."

Daisy looked through the windshield at the one-story brick stand-alone building in front of them. It had a white front door with large picture windows on either side with empty window boxes for flowers built in below. There was a brick patio in front of the small building and a white picket fence that separated it from the sidewalk. A sign over the door, hanging off one hinge, read "The Toy Chest."

In her dreams, when Daisy imagined starting a little bakery of her own, it looked exactly like this little place. It was perfect. It was so perfect, tears sprang to her eyes as she smiled at the charming building.

Fitz had gotten out of the car and opened her door, offering her his hand. She took it as she stepped outside.

"Fitz," she gasped. "It's . . . it's just . . ."

She looked up at him beaming at her, his face pleased and proud as he pulled her through the white picket gate that opened onto a narrow brick path. When they got to the front door, he let go of her hand and produced a key from his pocket. He unlocked the door, pushing it open as a little bell rang cheerfully overhead.

He held the door for her so she could enter first, and she walked into the dim space, lit only by the waning sunlight. It hadn't been swept, so dust bunnies, packing peanuts, and rolled-up newspaper littered the dull, scraped, hardwood floor. It was a clean rectangle of a room, though, with exposed brick to the left and right, and three doorways straight ahead.

She approached them, exploring each. The first was a good-size closet, almost a store room. The second led to the back of the shop where there were two small rooms flanking a back door, and the third was a tiny bathroom. She ran her hands along the aqua painted walls that separated the three doorways, finally spinning to take in the whole space.

"You did this for me?"

Fitz, who still stood leaning against the doorway watching her, hadn't said a word yet. Now he cocked his head to the side and said softly in a low voice, "I told you last night . . . I'd do anything for you."

Daisy's face exploded into a smile, and she sprinted across the room to him, throwing her arms around his neck and letting him gather her against his chest.

In his wildest dreams, Fitz hadn't expected this.

He had hoped she wouldn't be angry with him. He had hoped she'd actually like the space he and Stratton had chosen without her input. He had even been prepared to cajole her a little—convince her that with his help she could do this. But the one thing he never expected was to be holding her in his arms, feeling the warmth and curves of her body pressed up against him again.

When she embraced him, she hadn't turn her face away from his, but, more intimately, into him. Her cheek lay against his chest, right under his collarbone, and he could feel the heat of her breath on his skin through the open V of his shirt. He tightened his arms around her, bending his neck just a little, until his cheek brushed her forehead and his lips rested right near the bridge of her nose. If he moved just the slightest bit closer to her, he'd be nuzzling his lips to her skin, but he stayed as still as possible, desperate not to break the profound closeness he felt while holding her.

His heart pounded, and he wondered if she could feel the vibrations through his shirt, if she could feel the rhythm that was beating out his feelings for her. Her fingers, laced around his neck, were still except for one of her thumbs, which grazed the short hair on his nape distractedly, making shivers run from his neck to his groin. He softly groaned as he felt himself react to having her so close to him, his body aching for more after missing hers for so many years.

If he had ever wondered, even for a second, whether his feelings for her had weakened, he was assured now—as they roared back to full strength, full vibrancy, full visceral life—that he'd been dead wrong. Fitz was as deeply in love with Daisy right now as he'd been when she was seventeen. And just like then, she wasn't available to him. Only this time *he* wasn't going to London—*she* was engaged to someone else.

Alex's voice whispered in his head, *She's not married yet*, and Fitz panted lightly, not giving himself a chance to reconsider what he was about to say, just letting the words fall out of his mouth, no matter what the consequences.

"I'm throwing my hat in the ring," he whispered.

"Mmm?" she murmured, the sound reverberating from his chest to his throat where it kicked his pulse up a notch.

"You haven't gotten married yet."

"No."

"I'm throwing my hat in the ring," he repeated, a little firmer, a little louder.

"Wait. *What*? What did you say?" She jerked back from him, but he kept his arms around her, so all she could do was flatten her palms against his chest and lean back on his arms. Her eyes were wide and wild as she searched his, and it was all he could do to not lean forward and kiss her like the world was ending.

"I don't want you to marry Dr. M." He wet his lips, his heart beating impossibly faster. "I want you to marry me."

"You're out of your mind," she answered, and her face, which had been shocked a moment before, seemed to harden before his eyes. "We haven't seen each other in over nine years."

"It doesn't matter. He's not right for you, and you know it. The way he talks to you? The way he just left you here? You don't light up around him, Daisy. I don't know why you're settling for him, but I—"

"You and I have enough baggage to fill fifty airport carousels."

"So let's start unpacking."

"You *cannot* ask me to marry you again," she panicked, her eyes stricken.

"I can. I just did."

"Fitz . . . This doesn't make any sense."

"It does to me. It made sense the second my eyes slammed into yours last night."

"We barely know each other anymore."

"That's not true at all."

"Stop. You don't need to do this."

Amazingly, she wasn't struggling to get out of his arms, as though she might actually be considering his outlandish suggestion, or maybe she was just too surprised by his words to pull away from him.

"You're wrong. I *do* need to."

"No, you don't! God, you don't *owe* me anything, Fitz!" she yelled at him and pushed hard against his chest. "You don't have to buy me bakeries and save me from bad marriages!"

She was so furious, he loosened his grip on her, stepping back, letting her go.

She put her hands on her hips, tossing her braid over her shoulder, her face screwed up with anger. "I forgive you, okay? Here and now, I officially forgive you for everything that happened, for getting me pregnant, for never coming to . . . You don't owe me anything. You don't need to do these things to make up for . . . You don't . . . Just . . . Damn it, Fitz."

Part of what she was saying broadsided him as he heard the truth in her words. For most of his adult life, yes, he'd carried around the weight, the burden, of letting her down. Doing something—*anything*—for her to make her happy would ease his guilt over taking so much away from her.

But that part of him was tiny compared with the feelings he had for her—feelings he had *always* had for her. Is that all she thought there was between them? Obligation? Guilt? Did she really believe he wanted to be with her only to make up for her pregnancy and miscarriage? Jesus, could she really not know how he felt about her? Could Alex have been right?

He searched her eyes desperately, but was disappointed by what he found there. Her eyes had filled with tears, and her cheeks were red as she tried not to cry. *Oh my God,* he thought. *She does. She really believes what she's saying is the truth.* The realization crushed him, made him feel sick and frustrated. A lot of emotions were fighting for space on her face, but they all added up to one devastating reality: she had no idea how he really felt about her.

"Just stop," she whimpered brokenly, turning on her heel to leave, but he had to say something. Saying that he loved her wouldn't ring true right this minute, so he held that back. But he had to let her know he wasn't giving up.

"Daisy!"

She pivoted to look at him. He clenched his jaw, unsmiling.

"This is our second chance. You and me. Right now." He paused, rubbing his jaw. "Fair warning that you can pass along to your *fiancé*: while he's gone, I'm going to do whatever I have to do to make you fall for me, Daisy. Whatever it takes."

With that promise lying like a challenge between them, she turned and rushed out of the bakery, leaving him standing alone, body humming, mind reeling, a casualty of Hurricane Daisy.

Fitz English had just proposed to Daisy Edwards for the third time in her life, and for the third time he'd made that proposal without the merest mention of his feelings for her, without a word about his heart or love or affection. She knew he didn't like the idea of her marrying Dr. M.—his fist connecting with Josh's nose last night had made that reality salient.

She swiped at the tears on her cheeks, walking purposefully down the street in the direction of the Haverford village green, as his words bounced around like missiles in her head. The ones that kept reverberating loudest, however, were the last ones: *I'm going to do whatever I have to do to make you fall for me, Daisy.*

Falling for Fitz? That had never been the problem. She'd fallen for Fitz at seventeen and never looked back. The problem was Fitz falling—or more accurately, *not* falling—for her.

She turned under the small stone arch, into the town park. The green grass was littered with fallen leaves, and she hugged herself tighter, realizing she'd left her jacket in Fitz's car. She kept walking briskly until she got to the gazebo in the center of the park, where she and Fitz had once made out until daybreak, lingering long after an evening concert in the park, kissing and touching each other, talking about their hopes and dreams long into the night. Pieces of that conversation floated around her, almost like she could hear their phantom voices from so many years before.

"*. . . But what do you want to do, Daze?*"

Be with you, she thought immediately, *leaning forward to kiss his lips. When she sat back, he was still waiting for an answer.*

"*I don't know. I don't want to be unhappy like my parents.*" *She sighed, resting her head on his shoulder.* "*They never have fun. They never say 'I love you.' I don't know if they ever really loved each other. And now my mom's moving out to California, and I'm going to stay here with my dad. It feels so weird and lonely. It makes me so sad.*"

"*Don't be sad,*" *he said, pulling her into his side and nuzzling her temple.* "*You don't have to be like that. You can make different choices.*"

"*Like having fun and saying 'I love you' every chance I get?*"

"*Sure.*" *He chuckled softly against her skin, rubbing her shoulder gently.*

She considered telling him then and there that she loved him, but he continued speaking too quickly for her to muster the courage.

"*But you should figure out what you want to do with your life so you know where you're going.*"

"*Like how you're going to London,*" *she said with a heavy heart. It felt like everyone she cared about was jumping on an airplane and leaving.*

"*Exactly. I'm going to study British law there. Learn more about the origins of our legal processes. When I come back, I'll finish out pre-law and hopefully get into a good law school. And then someday . . . someday . . .*"

He stopped there, and Daisy wondered—just for a split second—if she figured into the someday he was talking about, but he hadn't said anymore. It didn't bother her that Fitz was so pragmatic. In fact, in such a time of instability in her own life, Fitz made her feel safe, which was comforting. He felt strong and stable and deeply rooted. He was going to England for a year, yes, but then he'd be back and he would be the sort of person who made careful choices, who built a good life, who didn't divorce his wife after twenty years and throw away a marriage. His dependability was almost as much of a turn-on to her as her whimsy seemed to be for him. Couldn't he see how well they fit together? How well they complemented each other? Couldn't he be the one to whom she said "I love you" every chance she got for the rest of her life?

"Daisy?" His voice brought her back to the present, and she looked up to see all-grown-up Fitz standing in the archway of the gazebo like a mirage.

"Why, Fitz?" she asked in a tired voice, her eyes still glistening with tears. "Why would you ask me that?"

He flinched, and his eyes narrowed for a moment, searching her face, as though making a decision.

"Because I . . ." He sighed. "I care about you, Daisy. I've always cared about you."

"That's not enough for marriage," she said softly.

He fixed his eyes on her, worried but true. "Because no else has ever made me feel like you do. Because you're so beautiful, I can't look away. Because I can't bear for you to marry someone else."

Her breath hitched as he said these precious words. They were so romantic, Daisy felt her resolve weaken. It was the closest he'd ever come to telling her how he felt. But ultimately, jealousy and love weren't the same thing, and wanting her so someone else couldn't have her would be a terrible reason to encourage him.

"How long will your fiancé be gone?" he asked, still staring at her intently.

"A couple of weeks. Maybe a month." *Forever.*

"Then give me a month. At least let me help you with the bakery. Spend some time with me. Give me a chance."

"A chance for what?"

He clenched his jaw, taking a deep breath. "To pay my debt. To deal with baggage. To get to know each other again. To show you what I can offer."

Daisy sighed. These weren't the words of love everlasting she'd always hoped to hear from Fitz, but she had to admit—they weren't just about settling old grievances either. What Daisy loved most about what Fitz was saying was that it had everything to do with settling the past *and* considering the future. It was like he wanted to see what could happen between them if she gave them a chance, and, she had to admit, she wanted to see too.

"Daisy, if Dr. M.'s the one? The love of your life? The person you want to say 'I love you' to every chance you get? Then tell me to leave you alone. You've done it before, and I'll leave you alone just like last time. But if there's a chance—just a *chance*—for you and me? Come to dinner with me tonight, and give me a month to make my case."

Her heart thumped like crazy as she stared at him, locked in the intensity of his eyes, his use of her own words from so long ago not lost on her. She'd come home to settle things once and for all with Fitz English, and this certainly wasn't how she imagined things being settled. But her heart—her hopeful heart, which trembled with love for him—gave her no choice but to offer him a chance at her future.

"Okay," she whispered.

"What?"

"Okay," she said again, unable to keep her lips from quivering up.

"Really?"

"Fitz!" she exclaimed, standing up, starting to feel exasperated.

He closed the space between them in a flash, drawing her into his arms, burying his face in her neck and sighing into her skin. "Okay."

Chapter 6

"I still can't believe you," said Daisy, shaking her head from across the table, her eyes sparkling and excited over a big bowl of pasta and a glass of good Chianti. He could watch her forever. Heck, that was the plan.

"Which part?" he asked, grinning back as he twirled his fork through a pile of linguine.

While they had agreed to spend time together over the next few weeks to get to know each other again, Daisy had asked that they not discuss his impromptu proposal any further, though Fitz couldn't help teasing her a little. For Fitz's part, he wondered if spending time with Daisy meant being able to kiss Daisy and touch Daisy and drag Daisy to his apartment to make love to Daisy because just sitting across from her at a public place was enough to make him hard.

She gave him a look and picked up her wine. "The bakery."

"Can I admit something?"

"Sure."

"I thought you'd be furious."

Her sweet smile widened. "Why?"

"Don't women like input on major life decisions?"

Daisy shrugged. "I don't know. It's not like you plucked the idea out of the blue. Anyway, I downplayed it last night. It's been my dream for years."

"But you never pursued it?"

"I never meant to bake cookies for a living."

"How'd you fall into it?"

"Well, food always figured into the equation. I went to culinary school out in California, and my favorite part was working with the pastry chef. When Glenn and I graduated—he was my boyfriend at the time—he was offered a job outside Portland, in a little town called Wilbur, and asked if I wanted to move north with him."

Fitz clenched his jaw at the mention of Glenn, some guy she'd obviously lived with. It was crazy and irrational that he envied Glenn, hated Glenn, wished Glenn was dead, but he couldn't help it. "Then?"

"Well, I had trouble finding a job. I was a hostess for a little while at Glenn's bistro, but I kept finding myself in the kitchen, which eventually found me out of a job. I worked as a barista in a sweet little coffee shop for a while, and I was shocked by the number of people who came in midafternoon for a pick-me-up. A half-caf latte and a mini cupcake. Or a cookie and an espresso. It was the bite-size treats that went the fastest. I saw the market for them and started baking out of my apartment."

"You distributed them locally?"

"I did," she said. "I sold them to that little coffee shop. I sold them to a nearby bakery and a candy store in the adjoining town. They got really popular, and I didn't know anything about marketing myself, but I did know that if I had a website, I could take orders. So Glenn had his brother make me a website. I was so surprised the first time I got an order, but it was a woman who'd seen my cookies and had asked for my information. She wanted two dozen in the shape of umbrellas painted white and blue for a baby shower and sent to her in Yakima. I worked on those twenty-four cookies for two weeks and must have thrown away twenty batches before I got them right. Anyway, I packaged them up beautifully, took them to the post office, and sent them off. And I got sixty dollars and three new orders out of it."

"How long ago was that?"

"Umm. About three years ago."

"How many orders do you fill a month now?" he asked, swirling another mouthful of pasta onto his fork.

"Oh," said Daisy, sipping her wine as she did some math in her head. "Hundreds, I guess."

Surely he hadn't heard her right. She baked cookies out of her apartment in Oregon. "Come again?"

"I sell over eight thousand cookies a month. Give or take."

Fitz's jaw dropped. She had no MBA training, no business skills, no business plan. She baked cookies in her apartment and sent them to her clients from the local post office. He was ashamed to admit that he hadn't even researched the financials of Daisy's Delights before having Alex draw the loan. In fact, Alex had secured it against Fitz's private bank account, which left him responsible if Daisy ended up defaulting and made him the silent partner of her bakery. But the reality is that Daisy could have afforded a much larger loan than the one they secured. She wasn't a risk. She was a success, and her potential was almost wholly untapped.

"That's two hundred and fifty cookies a day."

Daisy nodded. "Yep. Remember that they're small. I have industrial cookie sheets, which means it's about ten batches. They each cook for fifteen minutes. That's not even three hours of baking. Most mornings I'm done by ten. There's time for cooling, time for decorating and drying. I wrap them in cellophane and ribbon, pack them up, and send them out by four o'clock every afternoon."

"And you do all of this yourself?"

She shrugged, grinning at him as she dipped a piece of focaccia into a saucer of oil. "Who else would do it for me?"

"An assistant. A horde of workers in an industrial-size kitchen." He stared at her across the table, impressed with her drive and initiative. "You charged $2.50 per cookie three years ago. Even if you never raised your rates in three years, that would be $20,000 a month, Daisy. That's not some little start-up in your kitchen anymore. That's a real business."

"Well," she said, "the $2.50 includes shipping and handling and cellophane and ribbons and all my expenses. It's really only about $12,000 a month, once you include bulk discounts, return customers, and freebies."

"Freebies?" he asked, screwing up his face at her.

"Sometimes I'll throw in an extra dozen. You know, if they've been nice to me." She looked at him across the table. "I know almost all my clients by name. I've gotten to know them."

She had a thriving business, a work ethic to die for, and a loyal customer base. She was a triple threat, and all she wanted to do was open a dinky little coffee shop in Haverford, Pennsylvania?

He took another sip of his wine, admiring this new side of Daisy. Intrigued by her. Hell, utterly fascinated by her. It was so goddamned sexy too—her natural business acumen—he thanked God that Barrett had fallen for Emily years before they'd ever met Daisy, or she would have been the nip to his cat.

"Can I ask you a question?"

"Sure," she said, bright eyes shining.

"You could make this a national business. Several kitchens and distribution centers all around the country. Daisy's Delights could be in every grocery store, every coffee shop, every Target in America. Do you ever think bigger?"

"Fitz, I work from 5:00 a.m. until 4:00 p.m. every day. I choose how many orders I fill and which don't interest me. For example, Daisy's Delights is on hiatus right now. I got to town on Thursday, and I won't go back to work until I find a place to live and settle in a little. I make over $100,000 a year so that I can live where I want and do what I want and have a little bit of a life. I never missed a play rehearsal or a choir practice, and when a friend wants to grab a drink, I say yes. Why do I need to make it any bigger?"

"You know who's conspicuously absent from this perfect life you're living?"

She didn't answer.

"What does Dr. M. think about your business?"

"He's a dentist, Fitz. Cookies aren't going to be an organic choice for him. He disapproves of sweets in general."

Dr. M. didn't appreciate the brains and beauty of this woman, because their careers were at cross-purposes? Man, he was even *more* of an ass than Fitz had given him credit for.

"So he isn't supportive."

Daisy's cheeks flushed, and she reached for her wineglass, but Fitz was quick and grabbed her hand before she could occupy it.

"If you were mine," he said in a low voice, gently stroking the soft skin of her wrist with the pad of his thumb. "I'd support you in everything. Do you know that?"

Daisy looked into his eyes, trying not to concentrate on the effect of his softly stroking thumb. She thought of how she'd only told him of her dream to open a bakery last night and how here she was today, eating pasta in an intimate bistro with Fitz, discussing her future. A future he was helping her secure right here in Haverford.

"Yes," she whispered, drowning in his eyes.

"Everything, Daisy."

She nodded, her tongue slipping between her lips to wet them. His eyes tracked her movement like a laser beam, and when he looked back up at her, his eyes were deep and dark.

"I'm dying to kiss you," he said softly, his thumb warm and hypnotic on her wrist. "Is that going to be allowed?"

His words sent a shock of pleasure through her, making her breath catch and her heart race faster.

"I don't know," she answered honestly, then remembered her sham engagement. "I'm not a cheater."

He nodded, biting his lower lip as he stared at her, and this time her eyes were drawn to his mouth, to the ridiculously sexy lips she'd fantasized about for all of her adult life.

"You're calling the shots, Daze," he said, turning her hand palm up and leaning forward to press his lips to the inside of her wrist. They were warm and soft, and after kissing once, he dragged his lower lip over the sensitive skin, tickling and teasing. She'd been holding her breath, but finally exhaled as her eyes fluttered closed, and she drew her bottom lip into her mouth to keep from whimpering loudly enough to draw attention. Her insides flooded hot and wet, and she squirmed in her seat, wildly turned on by his gentle, seductive ministrations. When his lips abandoned her skin, she opened her eyes and took a deep, ragged breath as he dropped his glance to her breasts, to the way they heaved and fell against her shirt, proof of her desire.

His lips turned up as he watched her, molding her fingers carefully around the stem of her wineglass before placing his elbows on the table and leaning forward.

"I've never wanted any one woman as much as I want you right now. Not even when you were seventeen, and I would have sold my soul for a taste of you."

Her mouth was open, and she closed it, trembling as she brought her glass to her lips. The bitter wine was such a poor substitute for having his tongue in her mouth, and she looked up at him just in time for him to see that thought flit across her face.

"Whatever it takes, Daisy. That was the promise."

She gulped again, purposely glancing away before she swiped the table clean with the back of her arm and offered herself to him on top of it.

She wanted him too. God, she wanted him so much. But while the future had been a safe conversation for dinner, they'd avoided talking about the past, and they really needed to. As she observed earlier, they had an awful lot of baggage between them. They couldn't possibly consider building a future together until all of it had been dealt with.

She placed her glass back on the table and sat back in her seat, searching his face. "If I let you do this, Fitz—if I let you help me put my bakery together—I want to make two things clear. First, I will pay back every cent to English & Sons. Probably a lot faster than you think. And second, this settles any obligation you feel you owe me. I know that you feel bad about what happened, a-about my pregnancy."

Her voice had lowered to the barest whisper, and she paused as tears pricked her eyes. She was shocked to see his eyes suddenly glisten too, and he swallowed deliberately, reaching for his wine and taking a bracing sip. She wanted to keep going, to make him agree that whatever guilt or duty he felt would be forgiven with this gesture, but she got stuck watching his face change, and suddenly nothing was more important than asking the only question circling around in her head.

"Did you want it?"

His nostrils flared, and he clenched his jaw, his wineglass suspended in midair as he stared at her for a long moment.

"Did *you*?" he asked.

Her shoulders slumped. "Part of me did."

He nodded slowly, placing his glass back down on the table.

"Part of me did too."

"Fitz . . . ," she gasped softly as a fat tear rolled down her cheek. She shook her head weakly, staring at him. "I didn't know."

"You were seventeen. It wasn't my decision. God, I held back saying so much in my letters to you because I didn't want to pressure you or make you feel like I had an opinion or . . . or anything. I just want you to—"

"But it was yours too." She bit her top lip as more tears joined the first. Finally she added softly, "*She* was yours too. It was a girl."

He gasped softly, blinking furiously at this information, wetting his lips with his tongue before dropping her eyes. "How do you know?"

"They offered to test her DNA."

He nodded, still staring at the table. He sniffed once, exhaled audibly before using his fingers to swipe the wetness from under his eyes. When he looked back up at her, they were still bright with tears.

"I'm so sorry, Daisy."

"Me too."

He extended his hand down the side of the table, and she placed hers in his, watching as he curled his fingers protectively over her knuckles.

"Thank you for telling me."

"Thank you for wanting her."

"We can have more," he said softly.

His words, which were sad and gentle and hopeful and defeated, tugged at her heart as no words ever had. Daisy was rational. She knew that a seventeen-year-old and a twenty-year-old would have been challenged to make things work, and maybe having a baby would have ruined them in the end. But he couldn't possibly know how many times she'd dreamed of their little daughter. At the time, she loved him so much, all she could wish for was another chance to carry his baby one day. And here it was. Her wish from so long ago was finally coming true. It was just so much more complicated than her adolescent dreams.

"Fitz," she sobbed softly, looking away, trying to draw her hand away.

"Whatever it takes."

"Please."

"Okay." He took a deep breath and sighed, offering her a small smile. "No pressure. Just a chance."

She gave him the bravest smile she could, relaxing her hand. It had been a hard topic to discuss, but at the same time it felt good. It felt *really* good to open that suitcase and repack it together. A little less baggage between them. He'd wanted her baby. He'd been willing to make it work. His letters from England had been aloof because he worried about pressuring her. Knowing all of this meant so much more than she would have guessed.

"Ready to go?" he asked, as the waiter dropped the check at their table and he placed several neat bills in the check holder.

She nodded, taking a deep breath, reaching for his hand for the first time as they left the restaurant to walk back to the car.

It was dark by the time they locked up the future home of Daisy's Delights and drove back to the gatehouse at Haverford Park.

They were both quiet on the short ride home, and Fitz wondered if Daisy was as lost in thoughts about their baby as he was. He couldn't help but picture an eight-year-old little girl with a blonde braid over her shoulder and sparkling dark blue eyes. She'd have been very beautiful and very loved by her young, inexperienced parents. But would he and Daisy have survived? The chances weren't good, and he knew it. They would have had a daughter, but they very likely would have lost each other. His heart clutched, grateful that the decision had been taken out of his hands.

"You know," he finally said as he turned onto Blueberry Lane. "You never finished what you were saying before. You said you'd pay back English & Sons quickly, and then you started to talk about my guilt and obligation."

"I know that's part of this."

"A lot smaller part than you seem to think." He rolled down his window for fresh air, a fall fire carrying the smell of burning logs on the breeze. "I do feel guilty about the pregnancy. About leaving you to go to London. About the miscarriage. I have always felt like I let you down, but Daisy . . ."

She had turned to look at him as he spoke, and as he pulled into her uncle and aunt's driveway, he cut the engine, leaving them sitting in the quiet darkness, broken only by moonlight and porch light.

He rolled his neck to look at her in the quiet of his car.

"To be clear . . . this bakery? Setting it up and helping you with it? It's far more about courtship than debt. You've told me there's no debt between us, and I believe you. I cared about you then, and I care about you now, and I want you to be happy. And yes, part of that is because I hijacked some of your seventeen-year-old happiness and I'd like to replace it. But so much *more* of it is because it's a way for me to let you know how I feel, and it makes me feel good to do something—*anything*—for you. And that's the way it's always going to be."

Her eyes searched his in the darkness, and he felt the mood shift between them as she cupped his cheek with her palm. "I want to believe that."

"You don't have to believe it today. I have a month to prove it to you."

She nodded, and a small smile crept up her lips, mesmerizing him, making him desperate to touch her. He closed his eyes, turning his cheek until his lips touched her palm, and he kissed her gently.

He heard her suck in a gasp for breath before lowering her trembling hand to her lap.

"Something else, Daisy." Her chest heaved lightly as her eyes met his. "When you're ready, call Dr. M. and tell him my intentions. I don't want you to cheat on him. But there's something between us, and it's big. It's held on for nine years, and it deserves a chance. And if you're going to give it a chance, I need to know that I can reach for you, that I can touch you, that I can hold you in my arms and lay you out on my bed. It's up to you, but there's a line I won't cross unless I know you're free to be with me." He cleared his throat because he wished he was the sort of man who would take something that belonged to someone else, but he wasn't. "You decide. You let me know."

She tucked her lips between her teeth, her forehead furrowing. Finally she released her lips with an intoxicating pop that made his blood rush south with startling speed, making him the slightest bit light-headed.

"Okay."

Her acquiescence surprised him, but then, all night he'd been making a study of her flimsy engagement. She might not have realized it, but earlier at the shop, she'd informed him that she didn't need him to save her from *bad* marriages, and at no point had she checked her phone like she was hoping for a text or phone call from her fiancé. Though he couldn't quite put his finger on it, something didn't feel right in their relationship, and whatever it was, Fitz was grateful because it made him hopeful that he had a genuine chance with her.

Daisy turned to open her door, and her movement snapped him out of his thoughts. He put his hand on her arm, suddenly panicked that he didn't have a plan to see her again.

"Tomorrow, come to the office for lunch? We'll discuss what comes next for Daisy's Delights, and I can have my secretary start ordering your equipment and everything you need to get started. Come at noon. We'll have all afternoon."

Daisy smiled at him, her eyes tracing his face with care and gentleness, and it made him long for her touch on his skin again. "Earlier today, you said, 'What I lack in love I make up for in business.'"

He nodded, watching her carefully, memorizing the delicate lines of her face in the moonlight of his car, feeling his heart swell with love for her such that he had never known.

"Nobody, not ever, has romanced me the way you have tonight. Whatever happens between us, don't undervalue that part of who you are, Fitz." She smiled before leaving the car and closing the door behind her.

He watched as she let herself into the house, staring at the door as the porch light went to dark and the bedroom that used to be Emily's was suddenly illuminated. There was nowhere else on the earth he wished to be at that moment.

"It only exists for you," he finally whispered into the silence before turning the key and driving home.

Chapter 7

One of the first things Daisy did when she and Josh arrived in Philly on Thursday was take her father out to lunch and find a reliable used car to buy. And the second she saw the bright red VW Bug with only twenty-one thousand miles, she was sold. It wasn't a vintage model, which her father advised her could be costly for repairs, but it *was* a convertible, and something about buying a shiny red convertible Bug made Daisy feel as though a new life was really beginning.

As she drove the thirty minutes to downtown Philadelphia in the warm, late-morning sun, she realized how right that premonition had been. Over the past two days, she'd reunited with the love of her life and he'd found her a place to open a new business, and now she was headed to meet him to iron out the details.

For the first time in too many years to count, Daisy's life felt hopeful. Just being around her father and family had eliminated a good portion of the loneliness that had been her companion these many years far from home. And though she worried about protecting herself against heartache where Fitz was concerned, after he had dropped her off last night, she'd had time to review what was happening between them.

Most affecting of all was that he had been so clearly grieved about their tiny daughter, something she would never have suspected. It gave her insight into the man who was Fitz English, who would cry over a baby barely formed, lost almost ten years ago. How much of who he was, what he felt, what he wanted, was carefully concealed until it tumbled out accidentally? After she moved to California, to be with her mother, she'd destroyed the six letters he'd sent to her during the six weeks he was in London because they were so impersonal, and to her teen eyes, which clamored for words of love undying and passion everlasting, they were painful. She wished she still had them now to review them for subtle clues about what he had felt for her, what he had wanted for them. She might not have found anything, but embedded in words that had seemed perfunctory and dry to her, there may have been a bigger message, visible only to a more mature heart.

For so long Daisy had wished that Fitz was a different person—someone showy and passionate with his emotions and articulate in the declaration of them. But as she put the top down and let the warm autumn sun fall on her blonde hair, she knew that those adolescent hopes were just a fantasy she'd projected onto him. It occurred to her that maybe Fitzpatrick English simply wasn't given to emotive language, but that didn't mean he didn't own the feelings. The question was, what did Daisy need in her life? Did she require the words? The tender, passionate words in a lover's voice whispered into her ear? Or not? And was Fitz able to offer them or not?

Her cell rang in the console next to her, and she pressed the Bluetooth button on her radio.

"Hello?"

"Daze? It's Em."

"Hey, cuz."

"It's so loud. Where are you? The car?"

"Yeah. Give me a sec." Daisy hit the button to close the roof on her little Bug, waiting to speak again until the rush of wind had stopped. "Sorry. I'm back. What's up?"

"Uhhh . . . what's up with you?"

"Nothing much. Headed into the city. You?"

"Are you *sure* there's nothing going on with you?"

"You're speaking in riddles, Em."

"I was going to put the ring on last night, remember? Except my future mother-in-law was in a snit all evening because her son and my cousin pulled an MIA maneuver."

"Oh my God. We ruined it."

"Uh-huh. Again."

"Oh God, Emily," sighed Daisy, glancing at the GPS to make sure she was still headed to Fitz's building, on Arch Street near 30th Street Station. "I'm so sorry. Fitz wanted to talk to me. And then the bakery and dinner and the hat in the ring . . . sorry."

"I have to teach a class on the Lowell mill girls as an example of the exploitative nature of early-American industrialization in twenty minutes. Which means you have eighteen minutes to explain what a bakery, dinner, and rings have to do with why Barrett is going to have another torturous day wondering when his girlfriend is going to say yes to his proposal."

Daisy grinned. Every fiber of her being was grateful to be living near her cousin again.

"You know how I've always wanted to start a bakery? A little place that had baked goods and really, really orgasmic coffee?"

"Yeah."

"Fitz—well, actually, Fitz, Alex, and Stratton—arranged for it to happen. They found the most charming little pla—"

"Hold up. Hold up. What are you talking about? They *arranged* for it?"

"Fitz asked me on Saturday night what I was going to do now that I'm back, and I mentioned wanting to start a bakery. Last night, when we were walking up to Eleanora's, he said he wanted to talk to me. Turned out Alex approved a loan, Stratton tracked down a suitable place in Haverford, and Fitz did the rest. Permits. Contracts. Everything."

Silence.

More silence.

"Oh my God," murmured Emily. "He's *in love* with you."

"Emmy, don't be a moron."

"You mentioned you wanted to start a bakery on Saturday night, and Fitz bought you one on Sunday? Oh, that is *so* English brothers!"

Daisy smiled at her reflection in the rearview mirror as she waited for a red light to change. "Yeah?"

"Suffice it to say that Barrett pulled a lot of strings in my life to get me where he wanted in his. These boys leave nothing to chance, Daze."

"I think he's just trying to be nice to an old friend."

"No. No no no no no. It means Fitz is *into* you. *Really* into you. Really, *really* into you."

"Maybe," said Daisy, surprised when the word rolled so quickly off her tongue without arguing with Emily even a little.

"Okay, I have eleven more minutes. What was the thing about hats and rings, and why can I picture nothing but weddings in England as a result?"

"You're getting ridiculous now."

"Hey, I'm not the one with the brand-new bakery."

"I tell you what," said Daisy, not quite ready yet to tell Emily about Fitz's campaign to lure her away from her faux engagement to Dr. M. "How about we have a girls' night soon? And I'll spill everything."

"*Everything*? Even what happened that summer?"

Daisy took a deep breath. Emily had no idea that she wasn't just talking about a summer fling, but she felt ready to tell her cousin. "Yeah. Everything."

"Damn, I always *knew* there was something between you two that summer. Thursday night okay? Can Valeria come too?"

Daisy had met Valeria several times over the years, when she visited Emily and when Valeria and Emily came out to visit her twice in Portland. Daisy considered her a friend, and if she was going to really make Philly her home, she'd need a few go-to girlfriends.

"Sure. I'd love to see Val."

Emily gave her the address of a bar in Philly, and Daisy committed it to memory as she pulled into the parking garage under Fitz's building, promising one more time to tell Emily everything on Thursday night.

She hung up after exchanging "I love yous" and turned to the mirror again to check her makeup before leaving the safety of her shiny red car in exchange for lunch with Fitz English.

"Mr. English? Miss Edwards is here for you."

"Thank you, Gladys," said Fitz, taking a quick look around his office. It wasn't quite as big as his father's office, or Barrett's, for that matter, but Fitz had traded size for a corner view.

From his desk, set on a diagonal in the corner of his office, he could swivel in his chair and look out at his favorite part of the city: the campuses of the University of Pennsylvania and Drexel University, in addition to the 30th Street Station and the Schuylkill River. While attending UPenn, he'd crewed for the Campus Boat Club, and he still enjoyed taking his kayak down to the river on warm spring and summer weekend afternoons and spending a few hours on the Schuylkill.

He'd purposely left his apartment at the crack of dawn and arrived at the office by six thirty so that the majority of his work was completed by noon. He checked his reflection in the mirror over the burgundy leather sofa. His hair had gotten out of control in the past month or so and sorely needed a haircut. It brushed the top of his collar in the back and fell across his forehead in a wavy flop too often for his taste. He made a mental note to have his secretary schedule an appointment. He twisted the silver cuff links on his light blue dress shirt and straightened his tie, which was bright, fire-engine red and had a light blue repeat of bulls and bears. It had been a gift from Alex and was a little louder than Fitz's normal selections, but the bright red had grabbed his attention this morning.

He ran his fingers through his hair again and headed for the door, walking briskly through the long hallway to the reception area. He saw her through the glass, sitting in a guest chair, flipping through a magazine.

His heart skipped a beat as he stilled the hand about to push through the door so that he could watch her for a moment.

Her blonde hair was parted on one side, pulled back in a sleek ponytail. She was wearing a navy blue wrap dress with a V-neck that somehow managed to look sexy and conservative at the same time. Her long legs crossed at the ankles and were tucked modestly under her chair. He had a sudden, blinding flashback to those ankles locking around his back as he drew his body back from hers, then plunged forward into her wet, tight heat again. He gasped softly, holding his breath, feeling desperation overtake him for a moment. He couldn't lose her again. He couldn't.

As though she sensed him, Daisy looked up, catching him watching her. Her whole face brightened for him, blue eyes shining, lips spreading quickly into a smile that showed the whiteness of her teeth. She mouthed the word *hi*, holding his eyes through the glass while closing the magazine and placing it gently on the table beside her. Her eyebrows furrowed briefly, which didn't diminish her smile, but made him realize he was scowling at her. He blinked twice, forcing a smile as he pushed the door open.

"Daisy."

"Fitz."

He reached out to her, and she slid her smooth, white hands into his and stood up. Because he couldn't help himself, he pulled her toward him and leaned forward to press his lips to her cheek before stepping back. He dropped one hand, but not the other as he turned to Gladys.

"Gladys, please hold my calls for the time being. Miss Edwards and I will be discussing business in my office, and I don't wish to be disturbed."

"Yes, Mr. English."

Fitz turned to Daisy, tugging her hand gently back toward the glass doors, barely daring to look at her again until he could get himself under control physically. The overwhelming urge to lower her to his couch and cover her with his body was wreaking havoc on his judgment.

Lunch. Business. Business lunch.

He regretfully dropped her hand as he pushed open the door to his office, letting her precede him.

"Wow!" she exclaimed, walking past the sofa and coffee table and taking soft steps across the carpet to the floor-to-ceiling windows. "Wow. Just wow!"

He grinned, following behind her at a respectable distance, painfully aware that the woman of his wildest and best dreams was alone in his office with him.

"Nice view, Fitz!" she exclaimed, turning around to face him.

He drank in her pink lips and delighted smile, the way her blonde bangs feathered lightly across her forehead.

"The best view ever," he said softly, and she blushed. "I'm glad you could make it today."

"It's not like I have a ton on my agenda right now," she said.

"Are you looking for a place to live yet?"

"If I say yes, will you present me with a furnished condo by tomorrow?" she teased, following him to the small conference table in the windowless corner of the room, across from his office door. Two places had been set with linen place mats and napkins, silverware, and two dome-covered plates.

"If that's what you want," he answered truthfully.

"You don't owe me anything else, Fitz," she said, as he pulled her chair away from the table and she stepped into the void to sit down.

From behind her, he leaned forward until his lips were almost touching her ear and his breath brushed her skin like a kiss. "Courtship, not obligation."

He heard her breath catch mid-inhale and couldn't resist pressing his lips to the soft skin of her neck under her ear. She smelled like soap and shampoo and summertime, and his blood caught fire, coursing with liquid heat to his groin, which responded by hardening against the front of his suit pants.

"Fitz," she whimpered softly, and he forced himself to step back from her, touching the backs of her legs with her chair gently.

She sat down, and he moved quickly to the seat across from her to keep himself from touching her again. Her eyes were liquid and dilated when he looked up at her, and it made him harder under the table, his erection straining uncomfortably and making it difficult for him to form a coherent thought.

"I'm glad you're, um, here," he said. "We have a lot to sort through today."

She looked relieved as he started discussing business and nodded at him, leaning forward to take the metal cover off her plate. "Ooo! Caesar salad. This looks good."

"I didn't know what you liked for lunch."

"I like everything. I had to eat a little bit of everything in school so you can't really choose anything I won't enjoy. This is perfect, Fitz. Thank you for inviting me."

He grinned at her, taking the cover off his own plate and spreading his napkin on his lap. "Any second thoughts now that you've had some time to think through everything?"

Daisy wasn't certain if he was asking her about the bakery or the courtship, but she chose to focus on business and ignore the possible double entendre in his question.

"Nope," she answered brightly, spearing a piece of romaine lettuce and raising it carefully to her mouth. Daisy didn't have a lot of business clothes. She couldn't afford a big glop of Caesar dressing on her favorite dress. It was the exact same color as her eyes, and the few times she'd been asked out on a date in small-town Wilbur after Glenn left, she'd usually worn it. Unfortunately, none of the dates had led anywhere especially meaningful. Or maybe fortunately. Yes, fortunately. Because if any of them *had* worked out, she wouldn't be sitting across from Fitz now.

"Oh! I forgot to ask—can I get you anything to drink? Wine?"

She shook her head with a grin. "Not during the day."

He looked bemused, and she asked why.

"Because I can't remember you having many rules for yourself that summer."

"I had to grow up, didn't I?"

"I guess you did. And how well you managed it," he said in a low, seductive voice, flicking his eyes to the V of her dress, then slowly back up to her eyes, lingering for a long moment at her lips. "What other rules do you have for yourself?"

She'd flushed under his inspection and reached for her ice water now, savoring the cool glass as it cooled her fiery skin. "I wake up to bake every morning at five. I work out every evening."

"That's obvious," he said, licking his lips.

She rolled her eyes, ignoring him.

He chuckled lightly. "Okay, I'll stop. What do you do?"

"When I can, I bicycle outdoors, and I also have a stationary bike in my apartment."

"*Your* apartment? You and Dr. M. don't . . ."

"No," said Daisy. "We never . . . I mean, we don't live together. We didn't. In Oregon."

Fitz's face had hardened a little when he mentioned Dr. M., but now an interesting expression took over. "Another rule? About living with a man before marriage?"

"No. Not really. I mean, I lived with Glenn," she answered quickly and truthfully, realizing her mistake a minute too late.

"But not with your fiancé?" His furrowed eyebrows and ice water paused in midair cued her into how strange it sounded.

She scrambled to come up with a possible excuse. "I, um . . . I get up so early to bake, and um . . . and he doesn't open for business until, um, well, ten o'clock, and so . . ."

She dropped her gaze to her salad, which she started attacking with gusto. Damn it, she needed to be careful, or he was going to figure out that she had never been engaged at all. Would he be angry with her? Probably. He was going out of his way to win her when in truth he didn't have an existing rival anywhere on the face of the earth. Would he even be expending this sort of effort on her if he believed she was free?

When she looked up, he was still staring at her with those searing, searching blue eyes.

"Can we not talk about him?" she asked.

Fitz shrugged, reaching for his glass. "Sure."

Daisy sighed in relief, crunching on a crouton, hating that all the flirtatious comfort between them had been stamped out so quickly.

"No, wait," said Fitz. "I have another question."

Daisy placed her fork on the side of her plate and faced him, waiting.

"Did you call him last night?"

He was referring to his short speech last night about not crossing a line with her until she was free to be touched and taken. She shook her head slowly, and he flinched before dropping her eyes.

"Then I guess we should get down to business."

When Daisy left, almost three hours later, Fitz felt satisfied that they'd hammered out the orders for the equipment she needed and that they'd come up with a good plan for her opening in six weeks. She told him she wanted to manage the necessary construction: the two rooms in the back of the shop would be combined to create one large kitchen, with glass that looked out into the café area.

Again, he was impressed with her knowledge and clear thinking. Daisy had lots of ideas about the kind of oven she wanted, letting Fitz convince her to get her first choice—a top-of-the-line Bongard Cervap industrial oven with four decks, which meant that instead of making ten separate batches, she'd be able to do a whole day's worth of baking in two, and that included stock for the shop and all of her online orders.

Fitz had also urged Daisy to consider hiring a staff of three: two people to work the counter at the shop, and another baker to assist Daisy in the kitchen. He said that one of the two people working at the counter could also be responsible for packing up the online orders, and he encouraged her to think about automating her client list and opening a FedEx account so that she didn't have to go to the post office every day. They'd come to her and pick up the boxes at the same time every afternoon, eliminating another task from her long docket.

By three o'clock they were sitting side by side on his couch, looking at his laptop, shoulder to shoulder, their heads practically touching as he asked her what kinds of bistro tables and chairs she wanted.

Daisy sat back, propping her bare feet on his coffee table and leaning her head against the back of the couch. She turned her neck to look at him.

"No more decisions for today. My head is swimming."

He placed the laptop on the coffee table next to her feet and leaned back beside her, putting his arm around her and pulling her closer, up against the side of his body. When she bent her neck and let her blonde head fall on his shoulder, his heart thumped painfully with love for her, with hopes that they could find their way through the past and make a life together in the present.

Her forehead was nestled in the curve of his neck, and he leaned over and pressed his lips to her head, listening to her inhale deeply, then exhale, beside him, her swelling chest brushing into his side.

"This is nice," she said softly. "I'm so tired. I didn't . . . I didn't sleep well last night. I hadn't slept in Emily's room for a long time. Lots of memories."

"Any about me?"

"Mmm," she sighed. "Lots."

"Good or bad?" he asked, his lips still grazing the straight, soft yellow strands of her hair.

"A little of each," she said.

"Tell me some bad," he said gently.

"There wasn't much bad about you. I don't know if you remember, but my parents were divorcing that summer, and I'd stare up at the ceiling, listening to Emily's breathing and just wishing I didn't have to go home. My mother's and father's families had been best friends their whole lives, and I don't know why they chose each other. In a weird way it must have been like marrying a sibling or cousin. They fought like siblings. They weren't happy. My mother was moving to California, and I wanted to stay with my dad in New Jersey for my senior year. It was so depressing to think of going home."

He listened, putting their summer into a different context. He'd known, of course, that her parents were going through a separation, but she'd been so carefree, so full of fun and life, he hadn't given it much thought. Now he remembered the look on her face that night, when she said, "This is all we have left." He was headed to London for an exciting year of study and travel abroad. She was going back to a fractured home and the pressure of her senior year. Possibly pregnant. And he somehow thought giving her his high school ring would soften things for her? How stupid and naïve and self-centered he'd been. She hadn't needed a ring. She'd needed him, and he'd been thousands of miles away.

"I'm sorry," he murmured, pressing his lips to her head again and lingering there as his fingers tightened on her shoulder and his other hand reached for the one closest to him. "I'm sorry I wasn't there for you when you went home."

"We didn't know if I was—"

"I don't mean only that. You were going home to a heartbreaking situation. I could have—"

"No, Fitz," she said gently, squeezing his hand. "You were a kid, just like me. A student heading off to study abroad. We hadn't made each other any promises. I didn't expect that of you."

"But I should've been more aware of what was happening in your life."

"I didn't want that. I wanted to escape from my life that summer. You gave me that. You helped me not focus on it or let it own me. With you I wasn't someone whose parents were divorcing. I was just myself. You let me be myself."

"Tell me some good," he said quietly, lacing his fingers through hers.

"I already did. *You* were the good. I loved my uncle and aunt and Emily. But that summer? It was you. You were the good, Fitz."

His hand on her shoulder moved up to caress her cheek as he shifted his body slightly to face her better. She kept her eyes down, but he let go of her hand to push up gently on her chin. Her eyes swam with tears as she looked back at him. His eyes flicked to her lips as his breathing became heavier, then he looked back up into her beautiful eyes, which were dark and focused, searching his.

She clenched her jaw and swallowed. "I have to go."

He leaned back from her, nodding, still mesmerized by her beauty, by her generosity, by the way she made him feel like all the mistakes he'd made that summer were somehow okay. Letting his hand slip reluctantly from her face, he'd picked up her hand again and kissed it, whispering, "Whatever it takes."

She'd pulled her hand away slowly, then stood, slipping her feet into her waiting shoes.

"Have dinner with me tomorrow night."

"I can't," she said. "I'm spending time with my dad."

"Wednesday?"

"Fitz, this is moving really fast."

"I was thinking just the opposite. Thursday."

"Girls' night."

"Damn it, Daisy!" he exclaimed, jumping up and raking his hands through his hair.

"Friday," she said, walking to the door.

"That's"—he counted on his hand—"Tuesday, Wednesday, Thursday . . . three days!"

"See you then," she said, smiling at him before slipping out the door.

Chapter 8

Although Fitz respected her wishes not to get together until Friday, the flower deliveries had started on Tuesday morning with the largest bouquet of daisies that Daisy had ever seen, followed at lunchtime by hot pink gerbera daisies and a late-afternoon nosegay of light blue forget-me-nots. Daisy placed the blooms on the same makeshift table that held her paint cans and brushes, smiling at them every time she walked by.

On Wednesday morning, he sent wisteria, and their scent immediately sent her back in time to their summer together, as she remembered holding hands as the fragrant, hanging blooms blessed their heads while they kissed under Eleanora's wisteria arbor. When the door of her little shop opened again on Wednesday afternoon, her neck snapped up in anticipation to find he'd sent a dozen potted ivy plants, which fit perfectly in the empty window boxes in front of her shop. And on Wednesday evening, a simple clipping of lilac arrived, though they were so far out of season she could only imagine he'd had the single branch shipped specially from California.

A moment after the delivery van pulled away, her phone pinged with the arrival of a new text message from an unknown number that read, *Do you know what lilacs mean?*

Daisy's eyes widened. She opened an Internet window and quickly typed "lilacs meaning" into the Google search bar. She sighed when the answer came up: "first love."

Yes, she replied. *Though I have no clue what that has to do with us.*
I think you do.

Daisy's fingers trembled as she brushed them over the words on the screen. She stared at her phone, biting her bottom lip, wondering if she should reply, if she should push him to say it: I loved you, Daisy. Except what good would it do, when every passing day she didn't want those words in the past tense? She wanted them in the present tense. Before she could answer, her phone pinged again.

I miss you, Daisy. I'll pick you up at six on Friday.

Where are we going? she typed.

You'll see.

She huffed, staring at the words for an extra moment, then put her phone back in her pocket, adding the lilacs to the vase of wisteria.

Compounded by the fact that he wouldn't let her forget him for a moment, she missed him too. She missed him so much, she considered showing up at his office by Wednesday evening and telling him that she wasn't engaged to Dr. M. and all she wanted was to be with Fitz. But, despite his solicitous care of her since her return, she still didn't trust him entirely. She needed more time to be sure.

By Thursday afternoon, she'd changed the wall paint from aqua to light pink and painted the ceiling and all the trim in bright white. Her father had come by on Wednesday and sanded the front door and window boxes for her, and she'd already applied two fresh coats of paint to both as her displaced ivy plants sat dejectedly on the café floor, which wouldn't be refinished until after the construction had been completed.

The architect Fitz had recommended had submitted the simple plans for the kitchen to the contractor Fitz had also recommended, and she met with all of them late on Thursday, surprised when they said they'd already obtained town permits and would be able to begin the project on Monday. She suspected Fitz's hand in their amenability to prioritizing her job and marveled again at how he was able to let her feel in charge of everything while keeping tabs on everything running smoothly. She was grateful for his not-so-silent partnership.

By the time she headed home on Thursday afternoon, she'd totally forgotten about her plan to meet Emily and Valeria for drinks. Emily called around five to confirm, and Daisy waffled, considering canceling. On one hand, all she really wanted to do was draw a steamy bath and rest her weary muscles for an hour. But on the other, she relished the idea of going out with girlfriends because what she really needed was some good advice. She told Emily she'd meet them at seven and eschewed a bath for a quick shower. She quickly dried the wet from her hair, French braided it still damp, and threw on some jeans and a black sweater.

She was just walking into Mulligan's, a popular bar close to the UPenn campus, when she heard someone call her name.

"Daisy!"

She turned to see her cousin's roommate, Valeria Campanile, walking toward her and smiled. "Valeria!"

"It's been ages, woman!" Valeria opened her arms, giving Daisy a big bear hug.

"Since you and Emmy visited me out in Portland two years ago, I think."

"And you were with that guy . . . um . . ."

"Glenn."

"Glenn! Yeah!" Valeria held the door, and they walked in, looking from the crowded bar to the back, where they saw Emily's hand waving from a table in the corner. "Whatever happened to him?"

"Ugh," said Daisy. "Do you really want to know?"

Valeria shoved her way through the crowd, totally oblivious to the snotty comments and annoyed looks Daisy caught as she followed behind.

"Of course I want details!" Valeria yelled over her shoulder. "I've literally been studying for six straight years, and I've got the hips to prove it. Aside from the occasional mercy screw from a study group partner in the dark, I don't see much action."

Daisy chuckled in surprise, remembering Valeria's frank, genuine personality and why she liked Val so much.

They finally reached Emily, and Valeria slid into the booth seat beside her roommate, leaving Daisy to sit across from them on the other side. Emily started pouring beer from the almost full pitcher in front of her into the two empty cups on the table.

"Phew! I thought I might have to get into a fight to keep this table. I was getting some pretty menacing looks!"

"Am I late?" asked Daisy.

"No," said Emily. "I was a little early. And I have to tell you guys, Barrett might be stopping by a little later."

Valeria shot a look at Emily's finger. "I almost forgot! You didn't . . . ?"

Emily shook her head, looking up at Daisy, whose interest was piqued.

"What didn't you do, cousin of mine?" asked Daisy.

"She went to his office dressed in a trench coat today . . . ," said Valeria, ". . . and nothing else."

"Except for the ring in my pocket," lamented Emily.

"What happened?"

Emily sighed. "Just as I was about to open the trench coat and put the ring on my finger, Fitz burst into Barrett's office."

"No!" said Daisy.

"Something about a contractor who couldn't get a permit fast enough and he needed Barrett to make a few calls for it to happen. So Barrett asked me if we could get together tonight instead and picked up the phone to help Fitz." Emily took a deep breath, pursing her lips. "I stomped out of his office mad."

"And frustrated," added Valeria, grinning. She looked at Daisy over the rim of her beer glass. "A little tip: Barrett's office couch gets quite the workout. I'd avoid it if you ever have business there."

"Ew," said Daisy, cringing into her beer.

Emily rolled her eyes at Val before continuing. "Anyway, he texted me and said he was sorry he got caught up in business and could we spend some time together tonight. I said I was going out with you two. He said he'd just stop by later so he could take me home."

"For a long night of wall-banging sex," supplied Valeria helpfully.

"Val!" exclaimed Emily. "Barrett and I aren't all about sex."

"Um, I live with you, and he's over at least twice a week, and you're over there a least twice a week. Either sex is playing into things in a big way, or you're rearranging a lot of furniture."

Emily shook her head at her roommate, cheeks coloring.

"Come on," continued Valeria. "The walls are thin. Just sayin'."

"*Val!*" exclaimed Emily, swatting her friend on the arm. "Help me out, Daze. I suspect the contractor Fitz was so nuts about has something to do with Daisy's Delights?"

Daisy nodded, giving her cousin an apologetic look.

"I figured as much. And for your punishment, it's your turn on the hot seat."

"Yeah," said Valeria. "Barrett and Em are old news. We want to hear all about you and Fitz and whatever wild monkey sex you're having. God, he is so hot. What is it with that family? Every brother looks like Adonis."

"Have you met them all?" asked Daisy.

Valeria shook her head. "Not Stratton. But I've seen pics. He's hot too."

"But supershy," added Emily. "The elusive Stratton English. You'll be lucky if you ever meet him in person."

"A girl can hope." Val sighed.

"Wait a second! We're getting off course here. Daisy's supposed to be on the hot seat. Spill the beans, cuz."

"Refill us first," said Daisy, biting her lower lip.

Half an hour later, she'd told her cousin and Valeria everything. It was easy to speed though the story since they sat across from her with their jaws essentially resting on the table, frozen, except for the occasional "What?!" "No!" or "Oh my God!" Daisy would just nod and keep plowing through without stopping, worried she'd lose her nerve if she did.

Finally she sighed, looking Emily in the eyes. "So Dr. M. wasn't actually my fiancé. His name is really Josh. He's just a friend from my acting class who agreed to pose as my fiancé so I wouldn't have to meet Fitz again without moral support, looking like some pathetic middle-aged spinster."

"One, you're twenty-six. That's hardly middle-aged. And two, thank God!" sighed Emily. "Daze, I couldn't figure it out! He wasn't the right guy for you at all!"

Daisy grinned, relieved that Emily wasn't angry with her, and told them all about dinner on Sunday night and the bakery and Fitz throwing his hat in the ring and the meeting in his office on Monday, the endless flowers this week and fixing the contractor for her earlier in the day. By the end, they were sighing and loose-limbed, their faces soft and totally charmed.

"Daisy, I didn't know he had it in him," said Emily, reaching across the table to hold her cousin's hand. "He's always seemed so intense and . . . uptight."

"He is a little uptight, I guess," said Daisy, grinning at the girls across from her. "And definitely intense. But I sort of feel like I'm benefiting from all of that focus right now. Anyway, it always made me feel safe that Fitz was so levelheaded."

"Did he really cry? About the baby?" asked Valeria in a much softer and more contemplative voice than she usually used.

Daisy nodded. "He got a little upset."

"Why didn't you ever tell me?" asked Emily, tears glistening in her eyes.

"You were fifteen, Emmy Faith," said Daisy, using the nickname her Uncle Felix used for his daughter. "That would have been totally inappropriate. And then . . . well, I lost her, and I moved to California. I guess I didn't see the point in bringing it up later."

"I was so sad when you moved."

"Me too," said Daisy, squeezing Emily's hand as tears brightened her eyes too.

"I didn't know."

"Of course you didn't. No one did but me and Fitz. Even my dad never knew. I begged the doctor not to tell my dad I had miscarried. I don't know if he ever did, and I'd been released by the time my mom flew in the following weekend to help take me home. At any rate, my father never mentioned it."

"You were so alone."

Daisy shook her head. "No. No, I really wasn't. Fitz dropped everything and got on the first plane to New Jersey from London. He literally grabbed his passport and wallet, raced down the stairs of his dorm without packing a bag, hailed a cab, and went straight to Heathrow. He was by my side nine hours later. I woke up to his face on Saturday afternoon."

Daisy swiped at her eyes, remembering how anguished he had looked—his beautiful aqua eyes stricken and devastated. She should have known then how much he was hurting. She didn't. She'd read guilt, not love. But as she reached back for her memories and let them focus in her mind, she could see it in his eyes: the apology, the guilt, the sadness, and, yes, the love. It was all there.

"What now?" asked Valeria gently.

"More beer?" suggested Daisy.

"I'll get it," said Valeria, "but no talking until I get back. Swear it!"

Daisy and Emily nodded, giving each other uncertain smiles across the table once Valeria was gone.

"I kept a lot from you," said Daisy. "And I lied about Dr. M."

"Oh, I understand. All of it. I just wish you hadn't felt so alone."

"I don't now," said Daisy, rubbing her eyes again. "I'm really glad I came home."

"Your dad is too. He really missed you."

Daisy nodded. "It was hard to come home. Not just because of Fitz. I made a life for myself out there. The East represented hard times, you know? Sad times. I had to let go of those feelings before I could move home."

"Are you two talking?" demanded Valeria, plunking the pitcher on the table.

"No," said Daisy and Emily in unison.

"Just family stuff," Emily added. "I'm glad to have my cousin home."

"So!" said Valeria. "We're all caught up. What next?"

Daisy sighed. "I don't know. I mean, I came back home expecting we'd politely bury the hatchet, move on with our lives, and be cordial when we bumped into each other at family stuff."

"You still love him, Daze?" asked Emily.

Daisy looked into her cousin's blue eyes and nodded. "I never stopped."

"It doesn't sound like he did either," said Valeria. "But how long are you going to make him wait until you tell him you were never engaged?"

Daisy groaned. "Do I have to tell him?"

Emily nodded sympathetically. "'Fraid so. Can't start a life built on a foundation that includes lies. I mean, you're doing such a good job ironing out the past with him. You'd leave a fake engagement in the balance to bite you in the ass later?"

Daisy scrunched up her face, sipping her second glass of beer, then covering her face with her hands. "I guess not."

"We all need a refill," said Valeria, picking up the pitcher and refilling all three glasses to the top as Daisy mulled over her cousin's words.

"Cheers to Daisy," said Emily, raising her glass to toast her cousin. "I love that you're home. I love that you have a new business. I love that you reconnected with Fitz . . . but *promise me* you'll tell him the truth? That you're not engaged anymore? Just tell him."

"Yeah, Daisy," said a familiar voice from the end of the table. "Just tell him."

Daisy's eyes were wide and shocked when her neck whipped up, and they slammed into his, but as round and surprised as they were, they probably had nothing on his.

Fitz didn't care why. He didn't care how. All that mattered was that she didn't look destroyed and . . .

. . . *she wasn't engaged anymore.*

Thank God.

Thank God.

Thank God.

"Move over, beautiful."

She slid over slowly, staring up at him. "W-what are you doing here? We have a date tomorrow."

Fitz cocked his head toward Barrett, who sat down beside him, giving Emily a hungry look from across the table. "He invited me."

Daisy swallowed, looking anywhere but at Fitz, and finally noticed Stratton standing awkwardly at the head of the table, with his hands shoved into his pockets.

"Stratton!" said Daisy, her scattered nervousness immediately replaced with warmth in her honey voice as she leaned on the table and waved at the youngest English brother in attendance. "It's been a long time. It's really good to see you."

"Hey, Daisy," said Stratton, his rigid shoulders relaxing. And as if it was possible, Fitz fell even harder for Daisy Edwards's sweet heart and kind greeting to his socially awkward brother. Stratton may have too. Fitz almost scowled when Stratton grinned at her, showing off his little-known, panty-dropping dimples.

"You want to sit down?" Valeria asked Stratton, and Fitz looked across the table at her, noticing her for the first time.

He'd met Emily Edwards's roommate once or twice before, but hadn't really considered her until now because she wasn't his type. As he checked her out across the table, he realized that she wasn't bad-looking. She had wildly curly dark hair pulled up into some sort of messy bun, with escaped tendrils framing her heart-shaped face. Her dark eyes were wide and bright, and she had that olive-toned skin that looked tan year-round. She wasn't thin, but the extra weight filled out her face in a sweet, appealing way, and a quick glance below her neck told him it filled out other assets pretty well too. And right now she was staring up at Stratton like every drop of handsomeness in the English brothers' arsenal had been poured without reserve into him.

Stratton blinked at her. "Uh, yeah. Sure. You don't mind?"

Valeria shoved into Emily so hard she flew across the wooden seat and her hip hit the far wall of the booth with a thump.

"Not at all."

Valeria took over the conversation at a clip, and Stratton gestured to the waitress to bring over two more pitchers and three more glasses, looking slightly shell-shocked, but more comfortable than usual. Thanking God for Valeria Campanile and reminding himself to be available if she ever needed something from him, Fitz leaned an elbow on the table and turned his entire attention to Daisy.

"So . . ."

"So . . ." She sighed.

"You're not engaged."

She dropped his eyes and shook her head back and forth, reaching for her beer glass. He stopped her by placing his hand on top of hers and leaning down to whisper in her ear.

"Are you upset?"

"No."

"Then say it. I need to hear it."

She turned her head slightly, and their lips were so close that—if they hadn't been at a crowded table with his two brothers, her cousin, and Valeria—Fitz would have closed the distance. When she spoke, her breath warmed his lips.

"I'm not engaged."

"Since when?"

"Does it matter?"

"No."

He grabbed the hand closest to him and elbowed Barrett in the side. "Get out."

"What the hell, Fitz?"

"Now."

Barrett scowled at him and stood up. Fitz pulled on Daisy's hand, sliding her along the booth with him, until they were both standing at the end of the table.

"We'll be back in a few," he said over his shoulder as he maneuvered them into the crowd.

He'd been to Mulligan's more times than he could count, and he knew that in the back of the bar there was a long, dark hallway that had an alcove at the end where a pay phone used to be. Now? It was just an empty alcove. Without looking back at Daisy, he pulled her through the dense crowd of Thursday night drinkers, not stopping until he'd jerked back the curtain that still hung over the darkened doorway, pulled her inside, and yanked the curtain closed.

The red light from the exit sign just outside cast a pink glow over and under the curtain, and it was just enough light to make out her face looking up at his.

"Say it again," he said, his body on fire for her, hard everywhere, practically trembling with urgency.

"I'm not engaged," she whispered through shallow breaths.

He placed his hands on either side of her face, sighing with relief when one of her hands landed on his hip and the other reached up to hold his wrist. He told himself to be gentle, to take his time with her, but this was Daisy Edwards, about whom he'd fantasized for most of his life. And by some miracle, she was here in the dark with him, giving him the second chance that he didn't deserve, that he wanted so badly, it hurt.

His lips crashed into hers, their breathing mingling and quickening as his fingers firmly held her face and his blood coursed with purpose to his groin. Her fingers tightened around his wrist, and as she moaned into his mouth, he touched her tongue with his. As though electrocuted, she jolted, arching her body into his, and he pushed back against her until her shoulders hit the wall of the tight space, her body still bowed into his. He ran his hands down her neck, over her shoulders, and down her arms, winding them around her waist and flattening his fingers against her sweater where her back curved.

She raised her hands to his face, threading her fingers through his hair, moving her lips desperately, hungrily, beneath his, finding his tongue and sucking it into her mouth. His fingers curled into fists on her lower back, pushing her into him, wanting her to feel the hardness of his rampant desire and groaning when she rotated her hips just enough to let him know she wanted him too.

He kissed her like it was nine years ago, and like it was now, and like he'd never loved anyone as much as her. He kissed her like his life depended on it, because it did, and like he'd die if they stopped, because he might, and because he never wanted to live another day of his life unless it included kissing Daisy Edwards.

He trailed his lips down her neck, murmuring her name over and over as she leaned her head back against the wall, her breasts heaving into his chest with every breath. Her skin was soft and hot, and he loved the little sounds that she made in her throat, low and deep, that vibrated through his lips, sending waves of pleasure to the center of his body, where they pooled with want for her, hot and electric, desperate for more of her.

"Kiss me again," she panted.

He raised his head to capture her lips with his to nip and suck lightly while kneading her back. Her tongue swirled into his mouth, and he caught it, sucking on it as she wound her hands around his neck, lacing them against his skin, making him shiver and pull her closer.

When she pulled away to rest her forehead on his shoulder, he leaned down to caress her ear with his breath.

"I'm picking you up at six tomorrow," he whispered, like he needed to say it, like he needed to tell her that tomorrow would be an extension of now, of here, of more.

"What are we doing?" she murmured, tilting her head to the side to give him better access to her throat and moaning softly as his lips brushed against her skin. "What should I wear?"

Nothing.

"I'm making you dinner," he murmured, his teeth capturing the lobe of her ear as she gasped and trembled in his arms.

"At your place?" she asked, tangling her fingers in the hair that brushed his collar.

"Mm-hm." He drew back, looking at her face in the pale pink light. "Is that okay?"

"Yeah," she said, taking a deep breath and letting her forehead drop forward onto his shoulder again. "Yeah, it's okay."

"Daisy?"

"Hmmm?" she hummed against his shoulder, her voice kiss-drunk, soft and low.

"I'm crazy about you."

She moved her neck slightly to nestle more snugly into his shoulder.

"Me too," she finally answered in a whisper. "I'm crazy about you too."

It felt so awesome to hear her say it, he clutched her closer, as close as he could.

"You can stay over if you want," he added, nuzzling her hair, wishing that they didn't have to go back to the table, wishing they could stay wrapped around each other in a defunct phone booth all night long.

She leaned back, catching his eyes in the dim light. "We'll see, okay?"

"Okay."

"You go back before me," she said, reaching up to smooth her braid.

He grinned but shook his head. "I don't think so, beautiful. Unlike you, I'm going to need a few minutes."

"Oh," she said glancing down at where his erection was still pushed firmly against her belly. She straightened away from him, loosening her grip on his neck, letting her hands fall to her sides. "Is that better?"

"No. Not better. Terrible."

He sighed, and she grinned at him, wetting her lips, knowing full well that it made him crazy. He forced his hands to let go of her, despite the way his body craved more.

"Tomorrow night, Daisy Edwards," he said, touching his lips with his fingertips as she pulled back the curtain.

"Tomorrow night, Fitz English," she answered, licking her lips again before ducking out of the alcove, leaving him euphoric and frustrated and alone.

Chapter 9

Lying to her Uncle Felix and Aunt Susannah made Daisy feel bad, but it was better for them to believe that she was crashing at Emily's place, not having hot sex all night long with Fitz English.

Not that she had decided to have sex, hot or otherwise, with Fitz . . . yet.

Their kiss in the shadows last night had not taken the edge off Daisy's hunger—rather, it had increased her appetite level from peckish to voracious, but she was still trying to be sensible about their whirlwind reunion.

She sat on the bench under the old oak tree in the twilight, waiting for him to pick her up, her oversize purse holding a toothbrush and change of underwear, just in case. She picked a leaf off her short plaid-wool skirt and ran her fingers over her tan, V-neck, cashmere sweater. She heard an engine turn onto Blueberry Lane, but watched as a silver SUV zipped by the gatehouse, leaving her to her own thoughts for a few more minutes.

Fitz had changed quite a lot over the past nine years. He was much more expressive and open with her than he'd been before, his hot words of want sending shivers of pleasure down her spine just as much as his sweet words—*I'm crazy about you*—made her heart leap with hope and happiness. And yet his actions still dictated his feelings far more than his words. The way he'd done everything possible to secure a business for her, the way he'd been relentless about connecting with her since Saturday night.

Still, questions remained. Why hadn't he contacted her during all those painful years apart? Was it truly as simple as her telling him not to? That was a terrifying responsibility in Daisy's eyes. Had he taken her that seriously and literally because he was only twenty years old, bereft over the loss of their baby and guilt-ridden over Daisy's pregnancy and miscarriage? Or could he truly not discern between her emotionality and her true desires?

She said she wanted a bakery, and he bought her one.

When she asked if he'd find her a condo at her request, he assured her he would.

If—in a fit of pique—she told him she never wanted to see him again, would he suddenly move to Timbuktu?

It was too much power over one powerful person. She needed some sort of reassurance that adult Fitz knew the difference between her whims and wants, her true feelings versus brash words said in anger or sadness. She needed to know he'd push back if he didn't agree with her. She didn't want so much control over their relationship; she wanted a partner.

The deep growl of an engine pulling into the driveway and making a quick left into the small car park behind the gatehouse made a beaming smile spread out on Daisy's face. She leaped from her seat before he had a chance to cut the engine and sprinted to his window. He lowered it, looking up at her like the sun had just come out after a month of rain.

"Too beautiful," he said, by way of greeting.

She dipped her head and caught his top lip between hers, inhaling his surprised chuckle into her mouth and closing her heart around it. It was the sound of happiness, and she wanted to hear it every day for the rest of her life.

"Hello, handsome," she said, leaning back.

"You stole my chivalrous moment of opening your door for you. What if Felix and Susannah are watching? Want them to think your boyfriend's a cad?"

She stepped away from the car, her mouth dropping at the word *boyfriend*. He'd never even called himself her boyfriend that summer.

He exited the car smoothly, snaking an arm around her waist and pulling her up against him.

"Yeah, I said that," he said softly, searching her eyes before pressing his lips against hers again. "Any complaints?"

"Nope." Daisy leaned into him, savoring the hard warmth of his chest, letting the soft, firm pressure of his lips carry her away to a place where she and Fitz were the only people in the world. She wound her arms around his neck, playing with the waves that covered his nape.

"Don't cut this," she said, nuzzling his nose with hers as she pulled away. "I love running my fingers through it."

"Done," he whispered against her cheek.

That uncomfortable feeling returned, uncoiling in her gut when he answered her so quickly, feeding into her worries from before. She loved that he wanted to please her, but something about it didn't feel genuine.

Oblivious to her inner struggle, he took one of her hands from his neck, kissed it, and led her around to the passenger side of the car, opening it with a flourish. She sat down, pushing her worries to the side as he sat down beside her, grinning like she was magic, like she was the best thing the world had to offer and the world had offered her to him.

Just enjoy him tonight. Don't ruin this time together with worries.

He turned out of the driveway and headed back to Philadelphia.

"I don't even know where you live," she said.

"Well, you should," he answered, fiddling with the radio. "Everyone should know where they live."

Her eyes widened. "What does *that* mean?"

"It means I'm *not* asking you to move in with me right this second . . . but I *will* ask you someday soon, and it will be important at that point for you to know our address."

"Fitz, you're like a freight train."

"I swear to God, Daisy, with every other part of my life I'm methodical and careful. I look at every business deal from every conceivable angle, considering every risk and pitfall and problem. It drives my father and Barrett crazy because I hold up deals making sure I've looked over every word of every contract for future problems. I make very few rash decisions for English & Sons, and even fewer in my personal life."

"All evidence to the contrary, counselor."

He nodded. "I know. From where you're sitting, I probably look like the most impulsive person on the face of the earth. But I'm not. It's not my nature. It's you, Daisy. You're this place in my life where I can be spontaneous and a little wild and . . . I don't know . . . free. Yeah. You make me feel free."

It might have been one of the nicest compliments anyone had ever given her, and a lump rose in her throat as she realized how starched and monotonous his life must have been during the long years they'd spent apart.

"But you know?" he said thoughtfully. "I'm still me, even with you."

She sniffled, getting her feelings under control. "What do you mean?"

"Daisy's Delights is a solid business opportunity. It's not rash or crazy to go into business with you, because you're smart and talented and your business is already a virtual success." He flexed his hands on the steering wheel, staring out the windshield, not at her, as he added, "And I had nine years to sort out how I felt about you . . . nine *years*. It's not impulsive to want to be with you, Daisy. If anything, it's long overdue."

"Then why did it take so long?" she blurted out, wanting to kick herself as soon as the words left her mouth.

He was silent for several blocks, and she wondered if he'd heard her, but at the next red light, he reached for her hand and brought it to his lips.

"Losing that time with you is the biggest regret of my life, Daisy. The *biggest*, and you know that I'm not short on regrets."

"You never called. You never e-mailed. Never even friended me on Facebook."

He dropped her hand and stepped on the gas when the light turned green. "And you have no idea how hard that was for me."

"For *you*? You never looked back."

"I was *always* looking back."

"Maybe that's why you never reached forward!"

"Am I missing something here? You told me never, *ever* to bother you again. I honored that request."

"I was seventeen! I'd just lost my baby and broken my leg! I was scared and sad, but I *needed* you. And you said you'd *still* marry me, like you were doing me some huge favor." Her fingers felt tingly, and her chest tightened with her anger and upset.

He glanced at her quickly, then looked back at the road, his jaw hard and clenched. "Was I supposed to ignore your words? Railroad over them and fly out to California demanding that you see me?"

"Yes!" she exploded. "Yes! That's what you would have done if you had loved me!"

As soon as the words left her lips, she gasped, then turned her entire body toward the window. Fitz suspected she was crying, which killed him.

He fought the urge to yell back at her, taking a deep breath through his nose and trying to calm down.

"No," he said softly.

"Yes," she insisted, in a sob directed at the window.

"Daisy, I respected your wishes. I honored them. It would have been selfish to give into my own. My God, how can you not know this? I had to fight against calling you every day. Every single day."

"How could I not know? Because you never said a word." Her chest heaved with the strength of her heartbreak. "And I don't believe you. You didn't even have my number."

"I got it from the address book in Emily's purse when she left it in the vestibule on Boxing Day." He paused, remembering how he'd felt like a criminal for rifling through Emily Edwards's bag, but he couldn't have helped himself. He needed that bit of information, even though it had tortured him for years, the numbers seared on his mind at all hours of the day. "415–555–5234."

She gasped, turning her tear-streaked face to him. "What did you say?"

"415–555–5234." He bit his lip, turning into the underground parking garage at his building in Rittenhouse Square and pulling into his space as she stared with her mouth open. "I will never forget that number. I dialed it at least once a day . . . but then I'd hear your voice in my head telling me to leave you alone and I'd remember you didn't want to hear from me. It was my own selfishness that drove me toward calling you, and I'd hang up before pressing Send."

"Fitz," she sobbed, her shoulders caving forward in grief and surrender, her bottom lip caught between her teeth.

He held her eyes as steady as he could, while inside he trembled from what he was about to tell her. "I loved you. I *loved* you. I loved you so much, Daisy."

Her neck fell forward until her chin rested on her chest, and her shoulders trembled as she cried in the quiet of the car. The anguish she experienced as she re-sorted the past through his eyes made his lungs compress and his fists clench until they ached. If she was this grieved now, nine years later, how had she managed it at the time? The loss of their baby. The loss of her home. The loss of him.

He reached for the keys.

"I'll take you home," he murmured in a brokenhearted whisper over the lump in his throat. He had no right to her. None. How could she ever forgive him for how much he'd wronged her, for how much he'd hurt her, for how much he'd let her down? It was impossible.

She reached for his hand, pulling it to her lap, entwining her fingers through his. She took several deep, sniffling breaths before turning to him with red, glassy eyes.

"Whatever it takes, right?"

He didn't trust himself to speak. His eyes burned as he nodded.

"This is what it takes, Fitz," she said in a shaky voice. "This is what it takes."

He flinched, blinking at her as her lips quivered before tilting up a little, then a little more, until she was smiling at him with tears still coursing down her face. She shook her head softly, looking away from him before licking the salt from her lips and facing him again.

"You loved me," she whispered. A reconfirmation.

"Yes." He reached for her cheek, swiping the tears away as fast as they fell. "More than I had ever loved anyone in my life."

She took a deep breath and smiled again, with her red cheeks and watery eyes, nodding as though he'd answered an old, agonizing, important question for her. She hadn't known how he felt, just as Alex suspected. She'd never known how much he loved her. Why had he assumed she did? Did she have any idea how much he still loved her right this minute? Should he tell her? Should he—

"Okay. That's done."

"What? What's done? Okay, what?" He searched her eyes. A rush of panic made his thumb freeze on her cheek. Was this the end? Did she want him to take her home?

"Okay. You loved me. I can let go of that now. I'm ready for dinner."

"Just like that?" he asked, relief making his hand tremble lightly against her skin.

She covered his hand lovingly with hers, leaning her head to the side, smiling into his eyes.

"That's how this works, Fitz. We settle the past to clear a path to the future."

Daisy sat on a stool at Fitz's kitchen counter, forcing herself not to help him prepare their dinner. And she actually had to hand it to him, he wasn't doing a half-bad job.

He had chicken breasts already marinating when they got there, which he popped in the oven with two baking potatoes. And now she was watching him make a salad as they both sipped Yuengling out of long neck bottles.

Their conversation in the car had released a lot of tension for her, answering the most painful questions of their long separation. Hearing the words—*I loved you*—meant a great deal to Daisy, and it was as though they were healing and mending the patchwork of their past, sewing it back together piece by piece to make it whole again. She was even encouraged by him his disagreeing with her a little bit; it made her hope that he wouldn't just yes her in opposition to his own quiet feelings.

She looked at his bowed blond head, thinking that, as much as the English brothers looked alike, she'd never mistake Fitz for one of his brothers. His body was long and muscular and lean, and while he wasn't the tallest of the English brothers—that honor went to Stratton—he was well over six feet, edging out Barrett and Weston for third place. His jaw was sharper, his cheekbones higher, and he was altogether the handsomest of the bunch. And anyway, he belonged to her, and that made him totally unique in her eyes.

"Hey," she said, watching him cut up cucumbers. "Can you keep a secret?"

He looked up, offering a round piece to her. "What do you think?"

"I think so. But it's about one of your brothers."

She saw the feelings pass fleetingly over his slightly narrowed eyes—protectiveness and mild suspicion—before he seemed to consider the source and soften appreciably. "Let's hear it."

She grinned, popping the cucumber into her mouth and crunching. "Emily's ready to say yes."

"To Barrett?"

"No, to Dr. M. She felt so bad about me breaking things off that she—"

He was around the corner in a flash, his arms around her waist, yanking her off the stool—her back against his chest—as he bit the side of her neck in punishment. "You are *so* sassy. You were *always* so sassy."

Daisy had shrieked when he lunged at her, but now she relaxed in his arms, leaning her head back against his shoulder. He ran his hands slowly down her arms to her waist, spinning her around in his arms, then bending his head to kiss her.

The adrenaline from his sneak attack had already made her breathless, but now she melted against him, deliberately pressing her breasts flush to his chest and feeling her nipples pucker. Fitz slipped his hands under her sweater, sliding them slowly up the planes of her back as he deepened the kiss. She reached for the belted waist of his jeans, pulling on his crisp oxford shirt until she could press the skin of her hands to the hot, hard skin of his hips beneath, moaning softly at how good it felt and how much more she wanted from him.

"How much time?" she murmured. "Until dinner's ready?"

"Twenty minutes," he said breathlessly, letting his lips skate across her cheek to her ear, which he bit lightly, making her whimper and arch into him. She felt the soft vibration of his laugh. "Oh, wow. I just remembered how much you used to love that."

"Do it again."

He chuckled lightly, the tremors from his voice making goose bumps rise across her skin. He leaned forward, tracing the pink shell of her ear with the tip of his tongue, then flicking the lobe and making her whimper again. He caught the soft pillow of skin between his lips, sucking gently before slowly releasing it. Her breathing was ragged when he used his teeth next time, biting her gently, exhaling lightly near the damp shell of her ear, making tingles rush down her back as her knees weakened.

"Are you wet, Daisy?" he asked softly, amusement and arousal heavy in his voice.

"God, you're cocky."

But he knew her well. She was. She was wet and soft, and if he slipped his hand under her skirt, between her legs, he wouldn't need to ask.

"Tell me I'm wrong," he said, sliding his lips along the line of her jaw.

"You're not," she admitted in a low moan.

He growled as his lips crashed down on hers, demanding, consuming, ravenous for her, his tongue exploring every inch of her mouth as he cupped her ass and lifted her up easily. She locked her ankles around his waist as he started for the bedroom.

"Dinner?" she panted, kissing his neck over and over again, running her lips and tongue and teeth over every exposed bit of his skin, breathing in his soap and linen smell, knowing—with every fiber of her being—that this was exactly where she was meant to be, with Fitz, in his arms, loving him all over again.

"I want you under me for five minutes. That's it. I'm not spoiling this for later, Daisy. We've got all night. I just want to remember how it feels to have your body under mine."

He kicked open his bedroom door, walking into the dim space purposefully, falling on top of her as she landed on her back in his plush bed, keeping him locked between her legs as he rocked into her. Her skirt had ridden up in transit, and the friction of his jeans through her panties, arousing the throbbing, swollen skin beneath, was almost too much to bear.

She plunged her hands into his hair, her fingernails curling against his skull. Her back arched off the bed as she kissed him.

"Jesus, Daisy," he panted, pulling back from her, staring at her with fully dilated eyes. "Was it this hot?"

"I don't know. I don't remember," she said breathlessly, as he thrust forward. "Fitz . . ."

"What do you need, beautiful girl?"

"I . . . I need . . . I want . . ."

"You want me to touch you?"

"Mm-hm," she whimpered, biting her bottom lip as he rolled partially off her, just enough to slide his hand up her bared thigh. Daisy spread her legs just a little, her breathing shallow and ragged as his hand climbed higher.

"You're soaked," he whispered when he reached her panties, nuzzling her neck as he pulled her panties down to her knees and rested his palm over her soft curls.

She wiggled her knees to get rid of the lacy thong and pushed against his hand lightly, feeling his smile against her neck.

"*This*, I remember," he said softly.

With his fingers, he parted her lips gently, slipping one digit into the hot, slick valley of flesh and finding her clit immediately. Daisy bit down on her lip, exhaling an "ahhh" sound, ragged and rough, as he slid his finger up and down before pressing the flat of his finger on the button of nerves, making her flinch. Then he started rubbing faster, and Daisy felt the tightening, the gathering, the way her muscles bunched and the pressure built, spinning her higher and higher and higher until—

"Fitz!" she cried, falling apart against his hand, coming harder and stronger than she ever had in her life. It made her teeth snap and clench, and her fingers and toes curl. Her whole body shuddered and pulsed so fast, it was like one huge wave of pleasure. She had saved up nine years of longing for that one moment: it was the first time she'd climaxed with another human being since she was seventeen.

"Whoa," said Fitz, his voice close to her ear as she felt herself being gathered into the warm haven of his arms. "I definitely don't remember that."

"That was all you," she panted, her eyes still closed, her body like jelly, as latent waves of awesome still made her flinch and sigh in his arms. "All you."

He laughed softly, and Daisy heard the pleasure in the sound. It made her smile because he sounded happy.

"Are you okay?" he asked, pressing his lips to her closed eyes, first one, then the other.

Her eyes fluttered open, and she looked up at him, at the contours of his beloved face in the moonlight and streetlamp light and whatever light was filtering into his room from the hallway.

There was no trace of straitlaced, uptight Fitzpatrick English in the face of the man looking back at her. No clenched jaw or furrowed brow. He laughed quietly at the satisfied expression on her face, his blue eyes crinkled at the edges, full of happiness, soft with tenderness. Here in his bed, holding her in his arms, he was free and she was safe. That's what they had. That's who they were now and always had been. Except that now, as opposed to then, Daisy saw something more in his eyes, and it made her stare back at him with wonder. What Daisy saw—what she was *sure* she was looking at on his beautiful face—was love.

It wasn't just that he had loved her once.

He loved her now.

Right now.

She could see it. She could feel it. She knew it was true.

She turned into him and leaned up on one elbow to mirror him, her body languid and her eyes heavy.

"Fitz," she said, because it was—finally, finally—time. "I love you too."

It wasn't possible for him to smile wider. If he did, he'd strain something in his face, and it might stay that way forever.

"You do?" Not really a question. Just seeking reassurance to be sure he wasn't dreaming.

She nodded, looking a little shy, which was ridiculous after what had just happened between them.

"Have I told you that I love you?" he asked.

"No," she said, beaming.

"Really? I didn't mention that yet?"

"Fitz," she warned him, pushing him onto his back and straddling his chest.

He placed his hands firmly on her slim hips, pinning her with his eyes, holding her in place.

"Daisy Edwards," he said in a soft, low voice, overwhelmed by the strength of his feelings for her, "I am *completely* in love with you."

He watched the tears spring to her eyes as she blinked down at him. "You are?"

"I am, beautiful. I don't know how to be Fitz English without loving Daisy Edwards. I've belonged to you since I was twenty, Daisy. You've owned me every day since the last day I saw you."

As she stared down at him, two tears fell from her eyes to drip on his shirt. As gently as he could, without another word, he scooted her down on his lap and sat up, pressing his chest into hers, wrapping his arms around her and holding her tightly until the oven beeped a warning for the fifth time. Only then did he let her go.

Chapter 10

"Tell me something about you that nobody else knows," said Daisy, smiling at him from across the table.

Fitz shrugged, and his muscles flexed under his white undershirt. He loved it that she got distracted and stared at his chest for a second before reaching out with her bare foot and rubbing it against his.

"You won't tell me?" she teased.

"I'm trying to think of a good one." He took a long swig from his beer, staring at her. "Okay. Here goes . . . Since the summer we were together, I've never had a relationship last for longer than four dates."

Her eyes widened. "What? Get out!"

"I get to the month mark and lose interest. It's a running joke with my brothers, and it makes my mother nuts."

"So, you don't . . . ?" She flicked her eyes to his lap and back up again.

"What? Have I been celibate?" He grinned at her, feeling a little sheepish, not wanting her to imagine him with other women, but refusing to be dishonest. "Most women don't make you wait for the fifth date, Daisy."

To his relief, she didn't look upset, but she shook her head lightly in mock disapproval. "Boy, you must have quite the reputation for loving and leaving."

"Not for loving. I've never said that to anyone but you." He shrugged again. "And frankly, I don't really care. I'm not going to keep hanging out with someone if I don't feel anything. Anyway, it's hard to enjoy an endless buffet of hamburger when you've experienced filet mignon."

"Are you comparing me to beef?"

He winked. "To the very best beef."

She grinned at him. "What a crock. With all the rich, beautiful women in Haverford, that's hard to believe. I'm just a simple girl from Jersey."

"No one holds a candle to you, Daisy. Not for me."

She blushed, and even though the words were true, he didn't want to lose the lightness of the moment between them.

He raised an eyebrow at her. "And simple, my ass. You make calculus look like child's play."

She gasped, reaching across the table to swat his arm. "*You* were the complicated one. I was an open book."

"All right, open book, tell me something about *you* that nobody else knows."

She brought the beer bottle to her lips, sucking on it slowly and seductively, and, yes, it made him instantly fantasize about those lips wrapped around something else long and hard later.

"That orgasm I just had?"

Jesus. All she had to do was say the word *orgasm* and the perma-erection he'd maintained throughout dinner flinched in his pants. "Yeah . . ."

"It was the first one I've had with another human being since I was seventeen."

It was his turn to be shocked. And awed. And so goddamned turned-on that his arm actually pushed his plate to the side reflexively like he was clearing space on the table for them.

"But Glenn . . ."

She shook her head back and forth slowly.

"How long were you together, Daisy?"

"Three and a half years."

"How is that *possible*?"

"He wasn't very creative, I guess, or into pleasing me. He was a slam-bam-snore sort of guy."

"Christ, do I even want to know this?" He hesitated. "Dr. M.?"

"Are you sitting down?"

"As you see."

Daisy took a deep breath. "We were never engaged. We were never even together." She said it fast, cringed, then picked up her beer bottle and took a long, unsexy gulp as she watched him nervously.

Fitz's face registered shock, then confusion, and she watched as he sorted through some memories and thoughts, weighing things, reviewing things, before finally looking at her. His dark aqua eyes slammed unerringly into hers, and he didn't look happy.

"Damn it, Daisy, I *knew* it."

"Are you mad at me?"

"I'm a little confused. Why'd you do it? Why'd you show up with a fake fiancé?"

She looked down at her plate, away from the disappointment on his face. She wanted him to understand, but wasn't sure that he would.

"The last time I saw you, you'd come to my hospital room, and I perceived that you were grudgingly offering to marry me because you felt an obligation to me. Your letters from London had been sterile. And once you left that hospital room, you never looked back. That's how I saw things.

"When I decided to move back home, to be near my family, I knew it meant that I'd have to see you. Emily and Barrett are together, and there would be inevitable instances—weddings, baptisms, parties— where we'd both be in attendance. I just . . . The first time I saw you again, I wanted to look like I really had my life together. Sexy dress. Solid business. Respectable fiancé.

"I knew I still loved you, but I also believed in your indifference. I thought my feelings were something I needed to get over. I never considered that there was an actual chance we'd end up together. I just didn't want your pity or guilt, Fitz. I wanted you to see that I had my act together and that I wasn't irreparably scarred by what had happened between us. Having Josh by my side just felt . . . safer."

"Josh?"

"Josh Miller. Dr. M. He *is* a dentist. He's also a friend from my acting group in Wilbur."

"So it was about me. You fabricated an engagement as a buffer against seeing me again."

She nodded.

"God, you must have thought I was such an asshole."

"No," she said softly. "It wouldn't have been a crime not to love me. That summer was epic. And you were good to me afterward. Offering me a ring. Writing. Coming home when I was in the accident. Even saying you still wanted to marry me was your version of a stand-up move."

"No," he answered. "It was my crappy way of trying to hold on to you. I should have just told you I was in love with you."

Yes, he should have told her. No, he didn't. The twenty-year-old he was at that time hadn't been ready to tell her how he felt about her. He tried to show her, and she simply wasn't able to see.

"I should have seen," she whispered. "If I'd been older, or more mature, or not in crisis, I would have seen, Fitz."

"What did you say before? 'This is what it takes'?"

She nodded, feeling a little sad, but mostly relieved to be reconciling these long-painful moments, and finding out that the past could be left behind as they looked toward the future together. It was liberating, and though she might always feel sad that they missed out on years together, she'd always be grateful they found their way back.

"Hey," said Fitz, looking at her thoughtfully, "tell me this, what was with the way your friend was behaving toward you on Saturday night?"

She stared at Fitz, heat creeping into her face, feeling more than a little ridiculous about the whole thing. "He was being so weird and jolly about his dental practice. I took him out to the lobby and reminded him that he was supposed to be my fiancé. I was trying to inspire him to be a little more manly and possessive, you know? Anyway, we just performed *A Streetcar Named Desire* a few weeks ago at the Wilbur Country Playhouse. I told him . . . I told him to channel Stanley Kowalski."

Fitz sighed, dropping her eyes to look down at the table, and Daisy's embarrassment was complete until she noticed something: his shoulders were shaking. *Shaking.*

"Fitz?" she asked uncertainly.

He looked up, and she realized that he was laughing hysterically—so hard that he was making that high-pitched wheezing sound people make when the laughter bypasses the voice box. His whole body shook and trembled as he flattened his palms on the table to brace himself.

"Oh, h-hell, Daisy," he finally managed to say, through more wheezing laughter, "y-you definitely keep th-things interesting."

He took a deep breath and sighed. He was trying not to laugh anymore, but short bursts still escaped him, and Daisy wasn't sure what to do with herself.

She played with the label on her bottle. "He was pretty upset that you punched him, although I guess it convinced him that he's a pretty good actor, so he said to tell you that he forgives you."

Fitz launched into another bout of full-on, wheezing laughter.

"S-s-s-stop! P-please!" he choked out, using his napkin to wipe his eyes. After several moments, he was finally able to take a deep breath, and cleared his throat. "Oh, man, so I basically assaulted some poor guy who was just here for an acting gig at your request."

"Pretty much, Rambo," she answered.

His eyes cleared, and he stared at her from across the table, his lips still tilted up in residual amusement. "You know, I love you so much right this minute, I don't even know what to do with myself. I haven't laughed that hard in years, Daisy."

"You're not mad at me?"

"I'm not mad at you. I'm sorry you felt like you needed to do that, but I understand why you did." He pushed back from the table a little. "Come sit with me."

She got up and circled the table, letting him pull her into his lap as her legs dangled over the arm of his chair. She nestled into his arms, and he pressed his lips to the top of her head, lingering there for a moment.

"What's with you Edwards girls always posing as fake fiancées?" he asked, referring to Emily's "arrangement" with Barrett before they started legitimately dating. "Hey, speaking of . . . did you mean it before? About Emily finally saying yes to my brother?"

"Mm-hm." She nodded against his chest. "But we keep ruining it."

"*We*, like you and me?"

"Emily was going to tell him at the ball, but you punched Josh in the face. Then she was going to tell him at Sunday dinner, but we ran off and your mom was in a snit. Then on Thursday, she arrived at Barrett's office in a trench coat ready to put on the ring and take off everything else, but you burst into his office about the contracts for Daisy's Delights."

His mouth had dropped open as he listened to her, but then he cringed. "God, she must hate us. When's her next opportunity? We'll be on our best behavior."

"I don't know," said Daisy. "Sunday night? She said she wanted it to be special. She doesn't just want to just pop the ring on her finger while they're alone. She wants it to feel like a celebration or a declaration since he's had to wait."

"Barrett's had it bad for her forever."

"I know how he feels," said Daisy.

He shifted her in his arms so he could look into her eyes. "Do you?" She nodded. "Definitely."

The vibe between them had changed in an instant, and Fitz's eyes flicked to her lips before looking back up at her. "What do you want, Daisy? I want to hear you say it."

Her cheeks flushed with heat. "I want you inside me again. Now."

Fitz didn't bother kissing her at the table. He stood with Daisy in his arms and headed straight to his bedroom, her wickedly erotic words fueling the fire in his body, and he knew that their joining together was the only way to quench the flames.

"I'm not going to be gentle or slow with you," he said, his jaw tight and tense against her cheek. "I can't."

"I don't believe I mentioned gentle or slow when I just told you what I wanted."

"Jesus, Daisy! When'd you get so bold?"

She didn't answer as her tongue darted out and licked a line from the base of his throat to his chin, the firm pressure making his heart beat impossibly faster.

He strode into his room, backing up against the bed and sitting down so she straddled his lap. His fingers immediately moved from her ass to the hem of her sweater, which he pulled over her head without a word. She pulled at his too, so he reached back and yanked it off, then leaned forward to attack her mouth with his, plunging his tongue into the hot recesses without teasing, without courting or permission. She was his. And tonight, he was claiming her again after waiting almost a third of his life for the chance.

Her tongue met his stroke for stroke as his hands slid up her back. Finding no clasp on the back of her bra, his finger skated around the side to cup her breasts. They had changed since she was seventeen, fuller and rounder, but her nipples, which had always been sensitive, pebbled immediately for him as he brushed his fingers across them. Still kissing her savagely, he flicked open the tiny plastic clasp between them, and she moaned into his mouth, rolling her shoulders so that the straps sailed down her arms.

He groaned as his thumbs found her aroused nipples. Taking her lower lip between his teeth, he pulled from her until it slipped from his grasp, then dipped his head to her left breast. The full pad of his tongue brushed over the stiff nub of flesh before he pulled it into his mouth, soaking it with the hot wetness of his lips. She arched against him, her hands entangling in the hair on the back of his neck, whimpering as he sucked harder, finally releasing the bud to find its twin. She pushed his head to her right, moaning when he took her other nipple into his mouth, grazing it with his teeth before leaving a wet circle around it, feeling it pucker even tighter as he sucked it into a point.

"Fitz," she moaned, her nails digging into the skin of his scalp as he slid his hands to her sides and picked her up, setting her feet on the floor between his legs. He looked at her eyes once, which begged him not to stop as he reached for the waistband of her skirt, pulled down the zipper in the back, and bared her to him with one yank of his hand.

He seriously wondered if he was dead and already in heaven when she dropped to her knees naked in front of him. She reached forward for the belt buckle in front of her, opening it urgently before moving her fingers to the button on his pants. He tried to breathe normally as the zipper skated down with a quick *whish*.

She looked up at him, her eyes wide and black. "Take them off."

He stood up quickly and yanked them down, surprised when her hand reached up to alight on his abdomen and push him back down to a sitting position on the bed. She slid her hands up his legs, leaning forward into the V of his open thighs, then dipped her head. His breathing was so ragged and shallow, he had no idea how he maintained consciousness.

She took the base of his erection in her left hand and the rest of him in her mouth.

"Daaaaaaisy," he growled from the back of his throat like an animal.

Her lips slid down his shaft, and he clenched his eyes shut, the bobbing movement of her blonde head in his lap pretty much the most erotic thing he'd ever seen in his entire life. He panted, keeping his eyes closed and flexing the muscles in his thighs as she braced her palms against them for leverage. She released him with a quiet pop, then swirled her soft, wet tongue around his pulsing head, and Fitz felt himself swell against her lips. Damn it. He was too turned-on, too wired, too ready for her. He needed her. Now.

He put his hands under her arms, pulling her up, kissing her lips, tangling his tongue with hers and tasting himself in her mouth, which was pretty much the hottest, filthiest, most awesome thing he'd ever tasted.

"I want to be inside you, beautiful."

He slid back on the bed a little, reaching to open the bedside table and taking out a condom, which he ripped with his teeth and quickly fitted over his throbbing sex.

Daisy climbed on his lap, her legs around his waist, lifting herself just a little as he positioned himself beneath her.

"You're sure?" he asked quickly.

"I love you," she answered, lowering herself onto him.

"Oh God," he groaned, as the tight, hot, wet walls of her sex sheathed him until she sat on him, completely impaled. She exhaled, and her eyes rolled back in her head as she leaned back in his arms.

Her body was slick with sweat, and her nipples were tight and hard against his chest as he pushed up into her, then relaxed back.

"Fitz," she whimpered, wrapping her arms around his neck and resting her forehead on his shoulder as he pushed up again, feeling her tighten around him. It was like nothing else, viscerally fulfilling, so right and good, after he'd long given up the hope of sharing his body with her again in his lifetime. He was so deeply and profoundly in love with her, having sex with her was so much more than it could be with anyone else, and the memory of every woman who had come before or between his moments with Daisy faded into oblivion.

"I love you," he gasped, panting against her lips. "You know that now?"

"I know."

"I love you forever."

"I love you forever too."

He pressed his lips to hers, stroking her tongue to the rhythm of their lovemaking, as she pressed her pelvis closer to his, spreading herself against him so that he rubbed up against her mound with every upward thrust. He felt her flinch and throb each time, whimpering and moaning her pleasure into his mouth, higher-pitched and closer together as he moved faster. She was almost unbearably tight around his burgeoning, swollen sex, the friction between them tipping him over the edge of sanity. Her teeth bit into his shoulder, and her arms tightened around his neck as she started to come, her body arching into his, flesh to flesh, slick and hot and sacred.

She cried out his name close to his ear, contracting around him in waves that sucked him deeper into the recesses of her wet heat until she fell limp and exhausted against him, her panting breath teasing the dampness of his neck. Stronger and stronger waves of pleasure pulsed against him, building to a fevered pitch as she continued climaxing around him, and he gripped her hips, thrusting up into her once more, twice—

He clenched his eyes shut as stars burst behind them and the world melted away and all there was, was this. This sacred space. His whole life hurtling only to *this* moment, when the woman he loved was back in his arms again.

"Daisy," he growled, lifting her bowed head with his hands and finding her mouth to kiss long and deep as his body was racked with shudders, and he pledged his body, his heart, his very soul, to Daisy Edwards.

When Daisy woke up the next morning, she stretched, feeling beside her for the warmth of Fitz's hard body. Her eyes flickered open in disappointment when she realized she was alone, but the smell of bacon and coffee wafted into the room, and her mouth watered. He was making her breakfast. She smiled, sighing deeply in contentment, her words from so long ago drifting back to her:

Like having fun and saying "I love you" every chance I get?

Each and every time they'd made love last night, and innumerable times in between, Fitz reminded her of how much he loved her—not just in the way he touched her and treasured her, wrangling unfathomable pleasure from her aching body over and over again until she wept from the sweetness, but with his voice, with the simple words that she'd waited so long to hear. She swung her legs over the side of the bed, feeling the tenderness between her thighs, and she grinned, remembering all the ways they'd made love last night. On the edge of his bed, later on the floor, up against the cold plate glass windows— which had felt so filthy and yet so hot, she couldn't wait to do it again—and in the shower. They'd finally passed out from mutual exhaustion at three o'clock, nestled together like spoons.

Daisy used the bathroom, taking Fitz's navy blue terry cloth bathrobe off the back of the bathroom door and wrapping it around herself, even though it reached her ankles and she had to roll the sleeves. She loved the feel of it against her bare skin, and besides, it smelled like him. Plaiting her messy bedhead into a simple braid, she ran a washcloth over her face to pick up the last traces of last night's makeup and padded out of the room.

Oh. My. God.

He was standing with his back to her, remote in his hand, changing the channels on the television in the living room while something delicious crackled on the stove in the nearby kitchen. He was wearing only boxers, and her knees felt weak so she leaned against the hallway wall, staring at him hungrily, like they hadn't just gone four rounds all night long.

His skin was lightly tan, and she guessed he'd been supertan all summer to hold on to it now, two months after Labor Day. His legs and arms were insanely muscular and hard, probably from the crewing he'd done in college and the exercise machine on the floor of his bedroom. His shoulder bones flanking the straight valley of his spine made a perfect T, and his waist and hips were straight and strong, disappearing into his boxers, where a small strip of whiter skin peeked out. She sighed as she stared at his ass, remembering the muscles tightening under her fingers last night right before he came, pulsing and convulsing inside her body.

"Wow." She sighed softly, not even realizing she'd spoken until he turned around and grinned at her, crossing the space between them to pull her into his arms.

"Morning, beautiful," he whispered, leaning back so that he could press a quick kiss to her lips. Then he looked at her, his handsome face split by the smile he gave her, his sexy golden brown stubble in the morning light of his apartment making her sigh.

"*You're* beautiful, Fitz," she answered, and he kissed the tip of her nose.

Taking her hand, he pulled her toward the stools at the breakfast bar, pulling one out for her and circling around it to fix her a plate.

"Sort of thought you might be hungry after last night," he said, turning to grin at her.

"I'm starving," she answered, smiling back as he placed a cup of steaming hot coffee in front of her.

"Do you have anything you have to do today?" he asked with his back to her.

"I should find an apartment."

He turned around, placing a plate piled with bacon, eggs, and buttered toast in front of her. She reached for the fork he was holding, but he held it tighter. "You don't have to."

"Yeah, I do. I can't live with my aunt and uncle forever."

"Couldn't you . . ." His eyes were ridiculously blue and hopeful as he stared at her.

"Couldn't I what?" she asked, pulling on the fork until it gave.

"It would be insane," he muttered.

"Mm-hm."

"But we do insane so well."

She rolled her eyes at him, taking a piece of bacon off her plate and biting into it. It was crispy and perfect, and she moaned softly.

"I'm officially jealous of bacon. You make that same sound when I'm—"

Her cheeks flushed as her eyes met his. "You were talking about insanity, counselor."

He cocked his head to the side, looking at her thoughtfully. "I thought that case was closed."

"Did you already eat?" she asked, suddenly feeling nervous that she hadn't given him a resolute no.

"An hour ago." He watched her closely, eyes slightly narrowed. "So that case *isn't* closed?"

She knew that she should tell him that it was closed for now—she even heard the words in her head—but she couldn't quite form them, and he saw it on her face. The indecision. The possibility.

He planted his elbows on the counter across from her, leaning forward. "Imagine I'm standing below your window, throwing pebbles.

And you wake up to these pinging noises. And you know it's me, so you don't throw on a shirt or a robe—you go straight to the window and raise it. And there I am below you, smiling up at you and I say . . ."

"'Let's move in together,'" she whispered, locked in his gaze, mesmerized by the picture he'd just painted. He'd reversed their roles from so long ago, giving her a glimpse into his world, when she would seek him out, waking him from sleep with outlandish suggestions. "You always said yes."

He nodded, reaching across her plate to push a strand of blonde hair behind her ear. "Because it was you. Because you were beautiful and exciting and made me feel alive. Because I was in love with you, and I needed to give you whatever you wanted."

"But I need you to push back too," she said softly, "when my ideas aren't good, or when I want something that isn't good for us. I need you to still be Fitz English, who is so smart and careful and rational. I need to be sure that I don't change you from who you are."

"Are you worried about that?"

"I'm worried that you'll act impulsively around me and have regrets later. I'm worried you'll buy me a bakery and be annoyed by some of the decisions I make. I'm worried you'll ask me to move in with you and a week from now you'll resent all of my crap spilling out of the bathroom vanity and wish you'd thought it over longer," she said, reaching up to capture his hand and mold it against her cheek. "We've already had a lifetime of regrets between us. I love you too much to be too careless, Fitz."

"And I love you too much to be too careful," he said. "Daisy, you're like a drug to me in some ways, but like I told you last night, I'm still me. I don't feel like I'm making irrational choices. Going into business with you wasn't a risk. Being with you once you came home was practically an inevitability. Living with you? Let me be really clear here: after last night I'm not going to be able to go more than a night without sleeping next to you, and frankly, I'm dreading that night already. If you get a place, I'll be there three nights a week, and the other four you'll be here. Sharing a place just makes sense. Unless . . ."

"Unless?"

"Unless what I want isn't what you want. Maybe you want more space from me."

"I've had nine years of space. I don't need more," she said softly, turning her head to kiss his palm. "But moving in together so soon feels too quick and too crazy somehow."

He took a deep breath, his eyes unsettled as he dropped his hand from her face to refresh their coffee with a half-filled black-and-chrome

French press. She suddenly felt a small distance from him, and she didn't like it. It pulled at her heart and made her worried. She didn't know why she was being difficult. His apartment was gorgeous and only a thirty-minute ride to her café. Of course she wanted to move in with him. It was just that everything between them was happening at Mach speed, and she felt like they couldn't afford to make mistakes this time. This time everything needed to be perfect so that they wouldn't ever lose each other again.

He scratched his temple, meeting her eyes with the smart, no-nonsense look he probably wore constantly in the office. "Here's the deal. I've given it all the thought I need to. I can make the case. Or I can leave it alone. You tell me which you want."

She didn't know who was more surprised by the sudden smile that spread across her face with a soft laugh. He had an arsenal of good sense, of wisdom and judgment inside his head. She just needed to know that it didn't fly out the window from the strength of their chemistry.

"I love you," she murmured, holding his gaze, knowing in her heart that her children would smile back at her with those eyes someday.

And suddenly the stern concentration of his face softened as he grinned back at her. "I love you too."

"Don't make the case," she said.

He flinched, and his brows furrowed together lightly in confusion.

"Don't leave it alone either," she said.

He shook his head, his palms open, at a loss.

"Just give me a little time, okay? This—*you*—are too important to me to make big mistakes out of the gate."

"We're going to make mistakes, Daisy."

"I know," she said. "But we've earned a little clear sailing, haven't we?"

He took a deep breath and nodded, giving her a small smile. "Okay."

"Hey," she said, "you asked me what I was doing today, and since I'm going to put the apartment search on hold for now, what did you have in mind?"

His eyes sparkled. "Well, speaking of sailing, have you ever kayaked before?"

Chapter 11

Daisy told him she didn't know what hurt more by five o'clock: her stomach, which growled with the force of a hundred junkyard dogs, or her arms, which had not, in fact, kayaked before. Fitz told her that he refused to have sympathy for her, since it had been such a gorgeous, calm day on the water and he'd done most of the work. This had earned him a frown and a short-lived pout, which she reversed when he asked if she'd stay overnight again.

They stopped by Felix and Susannah's place so that Daisy could pack a quick bag, and Fitz called for Chinese at a place near his apartment where he had an account. By the time they arrived at his place, the food was waiting with the doorman.

They didn't bother setting the table, opting instead to sit side by side on the floor in front of the coffee table, eating directly out of the cartons, finally ending up sated and satisfied, spooned on the couch watching *The Holiday*.

"Jude Law is such a manwhore," said Daisy, who was lying in front of Fitz, with his arm draped over her hips. "He'd definitely play Alex in the English brothers movie."

Fitz chuckled into her neck, holding her tighter. It amazed him a little to realize that this comment didn't get his hackles up. For as much as he agreed with Daisy, he'd thrown punches at people for saying less about his brothers. They were fiercely protective of one another, regardless of how different they each were. But Daisy was so much a part of him, so much like family to him, she was on the special list of people who could say whatever she wanted to about his brothers.

"Apparently he used to follow us around a lot that summer."

The back of her head knocked into his chin when she whipped back clumsily to catch his eyes. "Ouch! Are you kidding me?"

"Nope. He told me last week," he said, rubbing his chin.

"Ugh. I adore him, but he is seriously disgusting." She made a revolted noise and then resettled in Fitz's arms. "How am I supposed to look him in the eye?"

"He said you were the hottest thing he'd ever seen."

"Oh yeah?" her voice softened appreciably. "So I could've had Alex English, huh?"

He threw a leg over hers and growled. "No."

He felt her stomach rumble with laughter and pressed his lips to her hair.

"Why do you think he does it?" she asked. "Do you think he really enjoys that endless parade of women? Don't you think he ever wants something deeper? More meaningful?"

"Honestly? Not really. I think Alex is Alex. He's always loved women; women have always loved him. He doesn't take them seriously, and they don't take him seriously. I think he's having a great time."

"Nuh-uh," she protested. "It's got to be lonely. He doesn't have *this*."

She wiggled her ass against Fitz's groin, and he bit back a groan. They were both exhausted, and yet it had been eighteen and a half hours since he last had sex with her. It was starting to take over his thoughts.

"Quit it," he said in a low voice, tightening his arm again, "or I won't be responsible for my actions."

She stopped wiggling, and he was slightly disappointed.

"I don't think Alex wants this," said Fitz softly, "though he doesn't know what he's missing."

"Someday someone will come along, Fitz, and she'll knock him on his ass. I just hope whoever she is, she can overlook his past, because if she ends up falling for him, she'll have to. Either way, she'll make him change his ways, you mark my words. She'll make him crazy."

"Like you make me."

She turned in his arms and pressed her lips to his. "Like you make me."

"I love you."

"I love you back."

"Move in with me?"

She took a deep breath and sighed, her lips still turned up slightly in the smile she'd worn since she faced him.

"Ask me tomorrow," she whispered, kissing him again.

She flipped back over to watch the movie, but he didn't feel like watching it anymore. He wanted to talk to Daisy. He wanted to hear her voice. And yes, he wanted to get her into bed.

"So who would play Barrett in the English brothers movie?"

"Barrett? The undisputed master of the universe?"

"What?" he asked.

"That's what Em and Val call him."

Spending a brief moment grumpily wondering why *he* wasn't called "the undisputed master of the universe," Fitz quickly remembered that he'd never aspired to it. He was happy letting Barrett be, well, Barrett.

"Okay. So who would play him?"

"Hmmm," she said, thinking. "Serious alpha male. Sean Connery. Pierce Brosnan. Daniel Craig. Someone strong and untouchable and perfect. Oooh. Maybe Aaron Eckhart. He's got that intense, strong-jawed thing going on."

"Oh, you must not have heard me. I didn't ask about me—I asked about Barrett," he said drily, then added, "And do you realize that, with the exception of Aaron Eckhart, you just named actors who played James Bond?"

Daisy chuckled, rolling onto her back. Fitz stayed on his side, braced on an elbow, his other hand flat on her belly as he looked down at her.

"Barrett is . . . intimidating, über–type A, intense. You're Fitz." She shrugged, smiling up at him. "You love me."

"I do," he said, leaning down to brush her lips with his, grateful even for that small intimacy and for Daisy lying beside him, casting a movie about his life.

"Okay. Enough about Barrett before I barf. Who'd play Stratton?"

Daisy sighed. "I adore Stratton. We logged a lot of hours reading side by side at the pool that summer. Best reading company I ever had. He never really lost the shy thing, though, did he?"

Fitz shook his head.

"You worry about him?"

Fitz swallowed, thinking about his younger brother, whom he loved so much. "Sometimes. I don't think he's ever had a girlfriend."

"Fitz . . ." She looked at him like he was being ridiculous.

"I'm serious."

And he was. Unless Stratton was incredibly tight-lipped about his college years, there hadn't been anyone. There'd been ample opportunity, of course, and Fitz had offered—many times—to be Stratton's wingman if he wanted to ask someone out. But Stratton had always smiled back and shook his head no, gently closing the conversation.

"Does he like women?"

"Yeah, he likes women," said Fitz defensively. "Hooking up isn't his problem, especially after a few drinks. Dating is."

Daisy sighed. "Well, to answer your question, I choose Ryan Gosling to play Stratton. He does shy really well."

"Another hot actor."

"Well, you can't fault me there. Didn't you hear that the English brothers are scorching hot?"

"All of them?"

"Especially the second one."

"I'm taking you to bed in five minutes."

"Then I guess I better get to Weston."

"I guess you better," he said, leaning down to lick her ear, "because he's not getting into bed with us."

"Alex Pettyfer," she said in a throaty voice. "Alex Pettyfer as Weston."

"I have no idea who that is," Fitz said, blowing on the skin he'd just licked and feeling her quiver beside him.

"Then you're missing out," she said, her eyes getting darker and needier. "Another scorching hot actor."

"Last question, who plays Fitz?"

"Fitz can't be in the movie."

"Why not?"

"Because someone would have to play Daisy, and I'd have to watch her kiss him. And I couldn't handle watching fake Daisy kiss fake Fitz. I'd want to hurt fake her for touching fake you."

"I belong to *you*, Daisy."

"You better believe it."

His hand slipped under her shirt, cupping one of her breasts through her bra, rubbing his thumb across the nipple until it was hard and Daisy was breathing faster beneath him.

He held her eyes and vowed, "No one's ever kissing me again, ever . . . except for you."

"It's been five minutes," she said, staring up into his eyes. "Time to take me to bed."

Daisy woke up at her regular time on Sunday morning, glancing at the clock on Fitz's bedside table, surprised to see that it was eight o'clock and he was still beside her, holding her naked body snuggly against his.

"You're finally awake." He sighed against her neck.

"So are you." She turned to look at him and had to bite back a moan. Fitz was always sexy, but first thing in the morning? With bedhead and a happy grin? He was crazy beautiful. "Why are you still in bed with me?"

"I woke up two hours ago," he confessed, his eyes profoundly tender as he gazed at her sleepy face. "But I asked myself, is there really anywhere else in the world you want to be right now? The woman you love, the most beautiful, most amazing woman on earth is sleeping next to you. Why would you want to go anywhere else? And so I watched the sun come up through the windows. I saw the way it turned your hair from white to gold over the course of an hour while I felt you breathe in and out against my chest. I closed my eyes and smelled your hair and memorized the feeling of your body in my arms, the way your legs entwine with mine. If I tried to pull away, yours were like magnets, following mine. So I kept them all tangled together, and yours were happy. Your back arches every so often, like it's making sure I'm still here, and your spine presses against my ribs, stealing my breath for a second, because nothing has ever felt like you beside me, and I don't want any more nights when your spine doesn't steal a little of my breath. There is nothing softer than the skin of your tummy and nothing warmer than the skin under your breasts, and you sigh in your sleep, did you know that? You sigh. And I decided it's the last sound I want to hear before I die, Daisy. I want to hear you. Sighing beside me."

By the time he finished speaking, her face was wet with tears, washing away nine years of pain with his beautiful words, which made everything better, which made her never, ever want to leave the heaven of his arms.

"Make love to me," she whispered, closing the distance between their lips and pressing her body flush against his.

He threaded his hands in her hair, parting the seam of her lips with his tongue and searching for hers. Daisy rolled slightly onto her back, and Fitz followed her, covering her soft body with his hard one, his erection pressing insistently against her softness as he gently ravished her mouth with his.

"I want you, Fitz," she whispered against his cheek as he kissed her throat, resting his lips against the throbbing pulse he found there. She grabbed a foil packet from his bedside table, tearing it open.

He rolled onto his back, and as she kissed him, Daisy rolled the condom over him quickly. She threw a leg over his waist, and without waiting another moment, she took the base of his erection in her hand and lowered herself onto him.

He flinched as his hardness passed through her aching entrance, reaching for her hips and holding her tightly. Her hands landed on his shoulders as she pushed back, taking more of him inside as he thrust up to meet her. Finally fully embedded inside her, his eyes open wide, he took a deep breath as she rolled her hips, moving at her own pace on top of him. She watched as his eyes dropped to her small breasts, which swayed lightly as she moved back and forth on him.

"There is nothing hotter than you," he murmured, staring up at her while his fingers bit into the skin of her hips. "You're a goddess, Daisy."

"I'm human. Touch me," she told him, and he moved one hand down the crease of her thigh to press two fingers into the swollen folds of skin. His other hand reached up to cup her breast, his thumb and finger rolling the nipple until it hardened. Daisy gasped from the combination of sensations, leaning back on Fitz, sliding back and forth on him faster and faster.

He grabbed her hips again, and she felt him thrusting upward now, joining her as they moved toward mutual pleasure.

"Kiss me," he panted, and she leaned down, gasping as her sensitive nipples met the hardness of his pecs. As their lips touched, he rolled, flipping her onto her back easily, holding his weight over her as he pumped into her harder and stronger. If possible, her body, which was already close to climax, clenched onto him tighter, aroused like crazy by his strength and possessiveness as he drove into her over and over again.

"More," she moaned beneath him, one of her fingers finding its way into her own mouth where she bit down on it. Her body felt stretched and sensuous, used and loved, the critical, fathomless pressure building below her tummy. "More, Fitz."

He pulled back almost totally, teasing her entrance with his tip, and she whimpered in frustration, every nerve ending wanting his thick heat filling her again.

"Look at me."

She opened her eyes, panting and desperate, on the very precipice of coming.

"I love you. Tell me you love me."

"I love you," she gasped, tears sliding into her hair from the corners of her eyes as she gazed at him.

His hips slammed forward, and the tip of his sex kissed her womb as her body exploded in shudders, convulsing around him, contracting and releasing, sucking him as deep as possible even as he collapsed on top of her, crying her name and telling her that he would love her until he died.

Fitz almost felt like he'd passed out from the strength of his orgasm, and it took him several minutes to realize that his entire body weight was resting on Daisy. His lips pressed against her neck, lightly sucking on her skin almost unconsciously as she continued to shudder with aftershocks beneath him.

"Daisy?" he panted.

"Yeah?"

"I should—"

He moved his hips, hating like hell to leave the tight warmth of her body, but knowing he needed to.

"Okay," she murmured, her fingers skating up his back to his face, which she cupped and lifted, looking into his eyes. Hers were surprised, dazed, like she couldn't believe the heat, the electricity, the intensity of the moment they'd just experienced together. "That was amazing."

"Are you crying, beautiful?"

She nodded.

"Why?" he asked.

"Because of what you said when I woke up. Because of how much you love me. Because I felt it—just now between us—how perfect we are together."

"We are," he said gently, pushing her damp hair off her forehead. "There's never been anyone for me but you."

"And you for me," she said, releasing his face with one hand to swipe at her tears.

"Move in with me?" he asked, leaning down to brush her lips with his.

"Ask me tomorrow," she answered, a small smile playing on the corners of her mouth.

"Am I getting closer?"

"Mm-hm," she answered.

"I won't give up."

"I know," she said, laughing softly as she cocked her head to the side, staring up at him with eyes full of love.

He braced one hand on the pillow beside her head and pulled out of her as gently as possible, swinging himself to the side of the bed.

His fingers reached down to take the condom off. "Let's go have brunch and then come back for round two in a lit—" Something didn't feel right. He looked down at where his fingers gripped the top and bottom of the condom, and with complete horror he realized it was empty. The tip had split in two.

"Oh my God," he panted, his heart kicking into an insanely fast rhythm that made his head swim.

"*What?*" she asked, leaning up and peeking around his torso.

"It broke. I don't know how . . . ," he started to say, but his words ebbed off as he got a look at her white, stricken face.

"Oh my God," she said, falling onto her back and reaching between her legs to the feel for the truth of his discovery. "Oh my God. Noooo. Oh my God. Oh my God."

She rolled away from him, off the bed, and bolted into the bathroom, slamming the door behind her.

He threw the condom in the trash and ran around the bed to the bathroom, knocking on the door. "Daisy? Daisy, are you okay? Come out. Please, beautiful. Please come out."

He leaned his ear against the door and could hear her muffled crying and the sound of tap water running. Finally, after several long, torturous minutes, the toilet flushed, and she walked out of the bathroom fully dressed, her eyes red and swollen.

Her expression was cold and closed, and she barely looked at him as she walked out of his bedroom without a word. Shocked, he stood naked in the center of his bedroom, completely unsure of what to do, before grabbing his boxers off the floor and pulling them on. He ran into the living room, grabbing her hand as she walked past him with her purse on her shoulder and her bag in her hand, headed for the front door.

"Daisy, stop! Can we please talk about this?"

"No," she sobbed, her granite expression splintering into agony. "No. This is just happening all over again. I can't . . . I have to get out of here, Fitz."

"Stop. Listen to me. Daisy?" He tried to pull her closer, and she didn't resist, but she didn't reach for him. She was limp, her back shuddering with violent sobs under his fingers.

"No," she said in a broken voice, then, "what?"

"Listen carefully to me, okay?" He leaned back and raised his hands to her face so he could hold it as he looked into her bloodshot eyes. "I love you. I *love* you, Daisy. And if our baby is growing inside you right now? I love that baby too."

Her face collapsed as more tears poured out of her eyes and she dropped her head. "No. No, Fitz. This is exactly what happened last time. I can't think. I can't breathe. I can't—"

He felt her breathing quicken until he started to panic that she was going to hyperventilate and faint. "Daisy, listen to me: This is *not* what happened last time. You are *not* seventeen, and you are *not* alone. I'm not going away this time. We're not scared kids. I *want* this.

This is all I've wanted for as long as I can remember. I've wanted to marry you since I was—"

"Stop," she begged him.

He winced, but to his relief, she sucked in a big deep breath. It was loud and messy, but she was at least getting air. She took another breath, then another, before stepping away from him, her head still down.

"I can't get my head around this," she said softly. "I can't—"

"You can. *We* can. It's a little messy, but it's also perfect. It's us, Daisy. It's our second chance."

She looked up at him with shattered eyes as tears streamed down her face. "I have to go, Fitz. I just . . . I have to go."

"I don't want you to go alone. Let me drive you home. I'm worried about you."

She took a sobbing breath and cleared her throat. "I'm okay. Don't worry."

"I'll come with you," he said, taking a step back to the bedroom to get dressed quickly.

She put a hand on his arm. "No. I need to go alone. You need to let me go."

You need to let me go. A vise squeezed his chest until all the air was compressed from his lungs, which ached.

"I love you," he rasped, blinking furiously as his eyes burned with tears.

"I love you too," she answered, sniffling and sobbing softly as she dropped his arm, walked down the hallway, and let herself out of his apartment.

When the door closed with a soft thud, Fitz realized he'd been holding his breath. He let it out, groaning as if he had the most painful—the most unbelievably painful—stitch in his side. He placed his hand over his heart, sliding to the floor before burying his head in his hands.

Chapter 12

Daisy hailed a cab in front of Fitz's apartment, her body shaking with shock and in chaos. Over the years, her brain had been able to dull what had happened between them so long ago, but when he said the words "It broke," just as he had that fateful summer night, every feeling—every frantic, terrified, heartbroken feeling—rushed back, assaulting her with such a fierce, unforgiving, pounding force that she could barely breathe.

It was too much—the past and present colliding too jarringly for her to process. Objectively, she knew that she was a twenty-six-year-old woman with a good business, a solid life, and a man who loved her. But in his apartment, faced with the identical words that had caused her so much heartache, she had reverted back to her seventeen-year-old self. She needed some space to remember that she was a fully grown adult who could handle things this time, but it felt like she could make that mental jump only on her own.

She rolled down the window of the cab, taking deep gulps of fresh air as her tears continued to fall.

What were the chances that this could happen again? Goddamn it!

She'd been so hasty when she put the condom on—she hadn't even bothered to pinch the end. She wasn't thinking about anything but feeling him inside her, feeling the pleasure and completeness of their bodies fully joined together. It was her fault this time. All hers.

Remembering the sick, desperate look on his face as she left made her take her phone out of her purse. She needed to give him some sort of reassurance, especially since she'd used the words "You need to let me go." It made her eyes burn all over again to imagine what was going on in his head, and she tapped on the messaging app quickly. Taking a deep, ragged breath, she opened a new text box on her phone and typed a simple message.

Fitz, it wasn't your fault. I just freaked out. I love you.

She pressed *Send*, then shoved her phone back in her purse.

Passing a CVS pharmacy, Daisy realized, for the first time, that she had a very real decision in front of her today. Unlike when she was seventeen and the morning-after pill wasn't available to her, it was now. She could easily have the cab stop, run into a pharmacy, and use emergency contraception to ensure that she wouldn't get pregnant this time.

If that's what she wanted.

I love you, Daisy. And if our baby is growing inside you right now? I love that baby too.

In a flash of blinding clarity, she knew that's not what she wanted to do. If Fitz's baby was growing inside her again right now—cells splitting and replicating and binding—she wanted that baby without any shadow of doubt. She pressed her hands flat against her abdomen and said a quick prayer that it was happening, that Fitz English's baby was already a reality in her body, even though she wouldn't know for sure for weeks.

She thought of the way he made love to her, the way he took every chance to reassure her that he loved her. The way he wouldn't give up asking her to move in with him. And she realized something else that she couldn't process earlier, in his apartment, when overpowering memories were crowding her head.

This is not what happened last time. You are not seventeen, and you are not alone. I'm not going away this time. We're not scared kids. I want this. This is all I've wanted for as long as I can remember.

She knew he was telling the complete and absolute truth. She wouldn't be alone this time. A few weeks from now, when she'd know for sure that they'd made a baby this morning, he'd be right by her side, as he'd promised. She knew it. She knew it with every fiber of her being. He loved her. He'd never let her down again.

The certainty she felt, combined with hearing his words in her head, made her start crying all over again, and she thought about asking the cab to turn around and go back to his apartment, but decided against it. It was like being drunk when they were together, and he probably needed a few hours of time for rational thought as much as she did. They could both do a little thinking about what they really wanted and then talk. Talk when? Tonight. Of course. She'd make sure he was coming to family dinner tonight, and they could talk afterward.

For Daisy's part? With every passing moment, she was more sure: she wanted to move in with him. She wanted to have his baby. She wanted to marry him and have a couple more.

She took her phone out again, disappointed that he hadn't responded yet, and opened another text box.

I'm sorry I left. I'll be at dinner tonight. See you there? I love you.

Then she put her phone back in her bag and rested her head on the window as the cab drove the rest of the way to her aunt and uncle's house.

Fitz wasn't the sort of person to mope around his apartment, but he indulged in a little moping after Daisy stormed out. He made himself coffee and sat on the couch where they'd lain spooned together, happy and carefree, the night before as she casted the English brothers movie. He stood in the doorway of his bedroom, smelling her scent everywhere. He finally picked up his clothes off the floor, surprised when his phone tumbled out of the back pocket of his jeans, battery dead. He plugged it in and decided to take a shower, where he did his best thinking.

He meant every word he'd said. He loved her. He loved their baby, if one was growing inside her right now. Just the thought made him blink furiously, grateful none of his brothers were around to call him a pussy for crying. That he and Daisy could be parents in nine months would be like a miracle, an answer to prayer, a dream, their second chance. Especially if she was his wife by then too.

What tortured him the most was the words "You need to let me go," which replayed in an endless loop in his head.

She had, for all intents and purposes, said the same thing so many years ago, when he told her that he still wanted to marry her. Well, actually, that time she'd thrown a ring at his head and told him never, ever to contact her again . . . but it felt terrifyingly similar, and he rubbed his burning eyes as hot water sluiced down his back. After finally having her back in his life, he couldn't lose her. He couldn't. He wouldn't.

Whatever it takes.

That's what he'd promised her, and her words came back to him: *That's how this works, Fitz. We settle the past to clear a path to the future.*

This was his chance to change the past. This time, he wouldn't sit back and be supportive as she scraped through this alone, making decisions on her own. He loved her. He loved that she might be pregnant with his child. She'd interrupted him before he could tell her that he'd wanted to marry her since he was twenty, not out of duty or obligation, but because that's how long he'd been in love with her.

He could change the past. He could. He would.

And it might take some time, but eventually she'd see that he wasn't going anywhere and she wasn't alone. He loved her, and he was never letting her go. One day, she'd believe that, and when she did, they could move forward again.

He stepped out of the shower, and while he was toweling off, he heard the light ping of his phone. Rushing into his bedroom, he grabbed it, checking out the two new texts. And his heart, which had felt so worried and grieved a few moments before, unclenched in a wave of relief.

He looked at the clock on the phone before setting it back down on the table to continue charging. It was almost ten o'clock.

Fitz had a few important things to do before tonight.

Daisy checked her phone frequently as the day wore on, but there were no messages from Fitz. And aside from feeling lonesome for him after spending every moment together since Friday night, she started to worry that (1) she may have lost him by running away, or (2) he may have taken her so literally, so seriously, that he was halfway to Timbuktu. She debated sending a message detailing the exact way she'd meant the words "You need to let me go"—i.e., she needed to get out of his apartment and think for a while, not break up—but she had also said "I love you" twice via text. He probably needed his space now as much as she had needed hers this morning, and she had no right to deprive him of it.

So she passed the day feeling miserable, watching the minutes tick by. By one o'clock, she couldn't stand the silence and drove into Haverford to visit her dad, who ended up taking her out for lunch at the Haverford Diner. They stopped by her new shop, and he told her how proud he was.

"Daisy-doo," he said, admiring her new pink paint, "the bakery's going to be just great. But if you don't mind my saying, you're not yourself today. Want to talk to your old dad?"

Daisy launched herself at her father, crying on his shoulder as he rubbed her back and maneuvered them both to the floor, where they sat, his arm around her.

"Oh, Dad. I'm in love with Fitz English."

"Well, that's old news."

"What do you mean?"

Her father shrugged. "He came to the hospital when you had that accident all those years ago. Stormed into your room while you were still out of it, told me he was your fiancé and he wasn't leaving."

"He was. My fiancé."

"And then he wasn't." Her father looked her straight in the eyes. "I don't know the details, and I don't want to, Daisy. But I know something happened between you two kids, and it's happening all over again now."

Her father had no idea how alarmingly exact his words were. He continued, oblivious to her own musings, pulling her against his bulky side.

"I figure some people are just meant to be together—poof. Just, poof! It happens. It's right. You can fight it, but you can't escape it. Wasn't ever that way for me and your mother. I'd known her since she wore diapers, and we still weren't right for each other. Your Uncle Felix sees a pretty girl painting in a garden outside Paris, and poof! Love story of the century. He writes to me two weeks later—he's married to Susannah. They been together for what?" He scratched his jaw, thinking. "Going on forty years now. And I think it's got to be like that for you and Fitz English too."

"I guess it is, Dad."

"You don't guess, honey. You know." He looked down at her. "It's written all over your face."

"I want to marry him."

"Well, nine years is an awfully long time to decide to say yes, but I have a feeling Fitz has been waiting for you, Daisy. Best not make him wait much more, eh?"

"Yeah," she said, grinning at her dad while her eyes swam.

Her father checked his watch. "We got an hour until the family dinner. Best head back to Felix and Susannah's place and dry those eyes."

They stood up and Daisy's father clasped her in a big hug. "Some people are just meant to be together, Daisy. Wasn't anything you could do. Plus, I never liked that dentist fellow anyhow."

If Mr. Edwards was confused as to why his daughter's head whipped back in shock, followed by a burst of surprised laughter, he was smart enough not to ask.

An hour later, Daisy walked up the driveway beside her father, aunt, and uncle, desperately hoping to see Fitz's silver car in the driveway, and her heart dropped when she didn't. *Maybe he's just running late,* she told herself, checking her phone for messages and trying not to lose hope.

When she'd gotten home from seeing her dad, she checked her phone to find one message from Fitz, which read, simply: *Okay*.

What did that mean? Okay, I'll let you go? Okay, I'll see you at dinner? Okay, I love you too? Okay, everything's going to be okay? She fidgeted with the zipper on her jacket. She was wearing skinny jeans, a white button-down shirt, and a tailored black cropped boiled-wool jacket with a velvet collar. She didn't want to overdress, but in case Fitz showed up, she wanted to look nice.

Eleanora greeted them at the door, ushering them into the massive front hall of Haverford Park. A ballroom-size marble floor was dominated by a grand staircase that split into left and right staircases on a half-story landing. Daisy flashed back to the first time she'd ever been inside Haverford Park. Fitz and Alex had invited her and Emily over for a movie. She didn't realize they were going to watch a first-run movie downstairs in the English family movie theater, complete with swivel chairs and a popcorn machine. Her jaw dropped when she finally understood the sort of stratospheric wealth of the boys who had become her summer friends.

"Why, Daisy," said Eleanora, smiling approvingly at her jacket. "How lovely to see you again."

"I hope I'm not imposing, Mrs. English."

Eleanora wrapped Daisy in her Annick Goutal embrace, and Daisy breathed deeply, telling her nose to memorize the smell of fifteen-hundred-dollar perfume.

"Not at all, dear." She glanced at Felix, Susannah, and Daisy's father, who lingered awkwardly behind. "You're family. All of you."

Daisy followed her family and Eleanora into the study, where Emily and Barrett sat side by side on the couch, chatting with Tom English, and she was surprised to see Alex, Stratton, and Weston all in attendance.

Alex, whom Daisy hadn't seen at the benefit last Friday, approached her immediately. "Hello, gorgeous!"

Daisy beamed at the charming Casanova, all but forgetting what Fitz had told her last night about him spying on them, dazzled by his panty-dropping blue eyes, which twinkled with constant mischief.

"Alex English," she said, "I bet you say that to all the girls."

He gave her a warm hug, but pulled back to grin at her. "But I don't always mean it."

"Hey, Daisy," said Weston, from behind Alex. She'd said a brief hello to Weston on Friday night, but she'd been so nervous waiting for Fitz to show up, she barely noticed how much he'd changed in nine years. She was right on casting him as Alex Pettyfer—he was brutally handsome, young, and buff, and if his older brother Alex didn't watch out, Weston would soon be giving him a run for his money with the ladies.

"Hey, Weston. When's the bar again?"

"February," he said with a wink. "Why? You need a lawyer, Daring Daisy?"

She chuckled lightly at the old nickname. "Not yet, but I'll keep you posted."

Stratton gave her a warm smile, and Daisy grinned back, but now that she'd said hello to his brothers, with no sign of Fitz, her smiles were starting to feel forced. Every English brother was here but one. The one she loved. The one she desperately needed to see.

"Need a drink, Miss Daisy?" asked Tom English, passing her with a beer in each hand for her father and uncle.

"Uh." She thought of her possible condition. "No, thanks, Mr. English. I'll just have some water."

She watched as he gestured to a young maid, then took a deep breath, looking around the room. Her father was talking with Tom and Felix. Susannah was sitting beside Stratton, who looked comfortable and relaxed as he did only with close friends and family. Weston and Alex were in the corner, probably trading tips about their latest conquests, and Barrett was on the couch talking to his mother on one side, with his arm around Emily on the other. Emily, whom Daisy hadn't noticed until now, looked jumpy. She stared down at her knees like she was gathering momentum to do something, and just as Emily started to stand up, it occurred to Daisy that her cousin was about to—

"Daisy Edwards!"

The whole room went silent as Daisy turned toward the sound of a familiar, beloved voice calling her name. She looked at the doorway of the room, where Fitz stood with his hands by his sides, unbearably handsome in jeans and a navy cashmere sweater, his blond hair tousled and his blue eyes focused unerringly on hers.

Her heart fluttered as a lump rose in her throat. His expression gave away nothing—he could be furious or thoughtful, anxious or determined. He didn't necessarily look happy, but he didn't look angry either. Daisy felt rooted to the spot where she'd turned to face him from the center of the room, her pulse speeding up as he approached her purposefully.

"I have something to say to you," he said when he was about a foot away.

No one in the room said a word. Daisy wondered if they were even breathing anymore, but she couldn't look around. She couldn't look away from Fitz, who had her utterly trapped with the intensity of his gaze.

"We're going to make mistakes. Do you understand?"

She nodded.

"But you're the person I want to make those mistakes with."

She told herself not to cry, but the tears snaked down her face anyway.

"I left you once because I thought that's what you wanted. But it wasn't what I wanted, and in the end, it wasn't even what you wanted. So here's a promise: I'm never leaving you again. Even if you tell me to let you go, I won't. I won't, because you belong to me and I belong to you, and I'll do whatever it takes to make this happen between us."

Daisy's eyes were distracted by a slight motion behind Fitz, and glanced over just in time to see her father's mouth go, "Poof!" She nodded once at her dad before turning her eyes back to Fitz.

"I want to have fun with you and run a business with you. I want to be the person you say 'I love you' to every chance you get, and you better believe I'll say it back every time. I want your legs to tangle with mine. I want you to steal my breath, and I want to listen to you sigh every morning for the rest of my life."

"Fitz," she sobbed, covering her mouth with her hands.

"I want you to move in with me. I want a family with you," he said, reaching forward to press his big, warm hand against her flat tummy. "But more than anything, I want you to be my wife. I've been in love with you for nine years. I love you more today than I ever thought it was possible to love another human being. So for the fourth time in my life, I need to ask you . . ."

He dropped to one knee before her, taking a small black box out of the back pocket of his jeans and opening it for her to reveal a sparkling diamond ring inside.

"Will you marry me, Daisy Edwards?"

Daisy started laughing and crying at the same time as she lowered her trembling hand from her mouth and presented it to him. He slipped the ring onto her fourth finger and snapped the box shut, standing up.

"Finally," he said, pulling her into his arms and lowering his head to kiss her like they were the only two people in the world.

It took a good thirty seconds for the rest of their families to explode in congratulations and clapping, coming forward to hug Daisy and Fitz, and Tom English called for the maid to crack open two bottles of his Krug vintage brut to toast his son and future daughter-in-law.

Through all the rowdiness of hugs and exclamations and congratulations, almost no one heard Emily Edwards's voice saying, "Excuse me!" until she picked up two lowball glasses from the bar and clanged the heavy crystal bases together, standing on a chair, a furious look in her eyes.

"Bar-rett!" she yelled from across the room.

Barrett, who'd been in the process of hugging Fitz, backed away from his brother, staring at his girlfriend standing on a chair, holding two glasses and wearing a frown, and the room went totally and completely silent for the second time.

"Emily?" Barrett asked, looking confused.

Emily's glance flicked to Daisy, and Daisy grinned at her cousin, whose faced softened as she beamed back at her. "Congrats, Daze."

"Thanks, cuz," said Daisy, leaning back against Fitz's chest as his arms folded around her. "Your turn."

Barrett crossed the room to Emily, who handed him the glasses, which he placed on the table beside the chair, then reached for her waist, pulling her down in front of him.

She reached into her pocket and pulled out the ring she'd worn as his fake fiancée and slipped it onto her finger, smiling into his eyes.

"Yes!" she said definitively, laughing as Barrett swept her into his arms and the room exploded all over again in congratulations.

Mr. English called down for two *more* bottles of champagne, Eleanora was already thinking of how to pull off two weddings in one year, and Felix stood proudly with an arm around his wife and another around his brother, accepting congratulations from the as-yet-unspoken-for English brothers. Daisy clasped Emily in a hug of pure joy, and Emily admired Daisy's ring while marveling over how similar it was to her own.

At opposite sides of the room, standing next to the women they would marry, Fitz and Barrett caught each other's eyes and smiled. Happiest of all were the English boys, who had loved the Edwards girls for as long as they could remember.

Their deepest wishes had finally come true.

THE END

The English Brothers continues with . . .

ANYONE BUT ALEX

THE ENGLISH BROTHERS, BOOK #3

THE ENGLISH BROTHERS
(Part I of the Blueberry Lane Series)

Breaking Up with Barrett
Falling for Fitz
Anyone but Alex
Seduced by Stratton
Wild about Weston
Kiss Me Kate
Marrying Mr. English

Turn the page to read a sneak peek of *Anyone but Alex!*

Chapter 1

There was something wrong with Alex English.

During his standing date with Hope Atwell in a deluxe suite at
the Four Seasons Hotel last Thursday, he had to force himself to
concentrate on the task at hand. While he grasped Hope's bare hips
and thrust into her from behind over and over again, his thoughts
drifted to work, to friends, to his family, to the Eagles, to the room
decor . . . for God's sake. Bored by her predictable moans and vulgar
compliments, he closed his eyes and finished the deed, but the entire
act left him feeling unsatisfied. Annoyed by Hope's banal postcoital
conversation, Alex used a nonexistent work meeting as an excuse to
leave her, and returned to the office.

At a birthday party last Friday night, Alex renewed his acquaintance with Juliette Dunne, with whom he had brokered two big deals
last year and enjoyed memorable sex on top of the boardroom table
at English & Sons to celebrate. After flirting with her for most of the
night, he'd followed her home, only to find himself distracted again.
As Juliette whimpered, "Oh God. Oh God. *OhGodOhGodOhGod,*"
taking a million years to climax, Alex wondered if it would be rude
for him to go ahead and finish without her, because aside from the
reliable physical rush he got from screwing someone, he wasn't feeling much else. After she'd finally yowled her way through an orgasm,
Alex quickly climaxed, but again, he was left feeling empty.

Feeling a woman shudder and tremble around him, calling his
name and clawing her way down his back usually made Alex feel
like the king of the world. Sated and limp, he'd contently stroke a
woman's naked back for hours while she prattled on about her life,

about her horses or kids or boss or backhand, waiting for an appropriate amount of time to pass before flipping her over and having her again. He had fun, she had fun, and after brunch the next morning and a long, sloppy, lingering kiss good-bye, he'd head for home with a bounce in his step, his mind already turning to his next rendezvous.

But his chest literally ached as he lay beside Juliette, who started talking about her latest deal. Numbers-while-naked should have been enough to make Alex instantly hard again, but all he felt was desperate to leave. Making the excuse of walking a dog he didn't actually have, Alex skipped out of Juliette's apartment at midnight and headed home alone.

Hoping to remedy the problem, Alex had ramped up his frequency and varied his partners the following week, adding—in addition to Hope—a tennis pro from the club, a hot cocktail waitress from his favorite hotel, a Junior League fund-raiser type whose husband was in Paris, and a Manhattan fashion model doing a photo shoot at the LOVE sculpture. All were beautiful. All were enthusiastic, compliant, and willing, and as an added bonus, the fashion model was surprisingly flexible.

The "something wrong" with Alex English?

Each and every time, after the deed was done, Alex didn't feel satisfaction or contentment or peace. He felt so hollow, it was painful, and it was genuinely starting to worry him.

At twenty-nine years old, Alex had enjoyed a solid fourteen years of getting whatever piece of ass he wanted, whenever he wanted it. And Alex had wanted it all the time. Young women, older women, married, unmarried, beautiful, plain, brunette, blonde, filthy, virginal, rough, and meek: he'd enjoyed them all ten different ways from Saturday and once more on Sunday morning before taking them to brunch. His reputation was infamous, and he'd heard every variation on his character: Casanova, Don Juan, manwhore, womanizer, heartbreaker, and among his friends? The Professor. Casual sex was Alex's forte, his living room, his favorite. He had no trouble procuring it, he performed like a god, and it always left him feeling awesome.

Until now.

After yet another lackluster date with Hope at the Four Seasons, Alex gave the matter some serious thought as he walked back to the office. He had hurt Hope's feelings this week—he could see the confused disappointment in her eyes when he left, after climaxing before *and* without her, then rolling quickly away. He'd made an excuse about work and kissed her farewell, but he couldn't get away from her fast enough—the emptiness turning to panic as he realized that this problem wasn't just going to go away by bedding more women. If anything, it was only getting worse.

As Alex walked the dozen blocks back to his office, he was shocked to realize that he could actually pinpoint the moment his troubles had started.

When his older brothers, Barrett and Fitz, had gotten engaged a month ago, as he watched Barrett with Emily, Fitz with Daisy, something happened inside Alex. His chest had started to ache. The pain was so sharp and unexpected, in fact, that as his father had uncorked a bottle of champagne to celebrate the engagements, Alex had slipped unnoticed from the living room to collect his thoughts outside. As he stood on the west terrace in the moonlight, palm pressed against his chest, sucking down gulps of cold, fresh air, he'd managed to convince himself that the ache was nothing more than some indigestion from the raw cheese his mother liked to serve with cocktails. It had nothing to do with Barrett and Fitz falling in love. He had rubbed his chest until the ache dulled to bearable, pasted a smile on his face, and returned in time for toasts.

But in the morning, the ache hadn't gone away, and its source was elusive and just out of reach. As the weeks went by, he realized it was a constant longing in the pit of his stomach, an emptiness that no amount of sex could fill, made fathomless by his efforts. He didn't have a name for it, but he hated the way it made him feel. Worse, he hated the way it was starting to affect his sex life. For the first time Alex could remember, sex on its own wasn't enough. He wanted—no, he *needed*—something more.

This frustrated him mightily because all he *wanted* was to get his life back to the way it was: regular, *satisfying*, casual sex with an oysterful of gorgeous women. That's what he knew. That's who he was. Because, hell, what was the alternative? Finding someone special? Making a commitment to someone? Monogamy, for God's sake? He shuddered. Alex didn't *do* commitment. Absolutely not. Not after what had happened in high school.

Look for *Anyone but Alex* at your local bookstore or buy online!

Other Books by Katy Regnery

A MODERN FAIRYTALE
(Stand-alone, full-length, unconnected romances inspired by classic fairy tales.)

The Vixen and the Vet
(inspired by "Beauty and the Beast")
2014

Never Let You Go
(inspired by "Hansel and Gretel")
2015

Ginger's Heart
(inspired by "Little Red Riding Hood")
2016

Don't Speak
(inspired by "The Little Mermaid")
2017

Swan Song
(inspired by "The Ugly Duckling")
2018

ENCHANTED PLACES
(Stand-alone, full-length stories that are set in beautiful places.)

Playing for Love at Deep Haven
2015

Restoring Love at Bolton Castle
2016

Risking Love at Moonstone Manor
2017

A Season of Love at Summerhaven
2018

ABOUT THE AUTHOR

USA Today **bestselling author Katy Regnery** started her writing career by enrolling in a short story class in January 2012. One year later, she signed her first contract for a winter romance entitled *By Proxy*.

Katy claims authorship of the multi-titled Blueberry Lane Series which follows the English, Winslow, Rousseau, Story and Ambler families of Philadelphia, the five-book, bestselling A Modern Fairytale series, the Enchanted Places series, and a standalone novella, *Frosted*.

Katy's first Modern Fairytale romance, *The Vixen and the Vet*, was nominated for a RITA® in 2015 and won the 2015 Kindle Book Award for romance. Four of her books: *The Vixen and the Vet* (A Modern Fairytale), *Never Let You Go* (A Modern Fairytale), *Falling for Fitz* (The English Brothers #2) and *By Proxy* (Heart of Montana #1) have been #1 genre bestsellers on Amazon. Katy's boxed set, The English Brothers Boxed Set, Books #1–4, hit the *USA Today* bestseller list in 2015 and her Christmas story, *Marrying Mr. English*, appeared on the same list a week later.

Katy lives in the relative wilds of northern Fairfield County, Connecticut, where her writing room looks out at the woods, and her husband, two young children, and two dogs create just enough cheerful chaos to remind her that the very best love stories begin at home.

Sign up for Katy's newsletter today: http://www.katyregnery.com!

Connect with Katy

Katy LOVES connecting with her readers and answers every e-mail, message, tweet, and post personally! Connect with Katy!

Katy's Website: http://katyregnery.com
Katy's E-mail: katy@katyregnery.com
Katy's Facebook Page: https://www.facebook.com/KatyRegnery
Katy's Pinterest Page: https://www.pinterest.com/
    katharineregner
Katy's Amazon Profile: http://www.amazon.com/
    Katy-Regnery/e/B00FDZKXYU
Katy's Goodreads Profile: https://www.goodreads.com/author/
    show/7211470.Katy_Regnery

CPSIA information can be obtained at www.ICGtesting.com
Printed in the USA
LVOW07s2241170316

479691LV00003B/3/P